Slippery When Wet

A Murder Mystery

by

Shelby L. Syckes

Foreword by Albert L. Feldstein

Copyright © Shelby L. Syckes 2019

All rights reserved. No part of this book may be reproduced in any form or by any electronic or mechanical means, including information storage and retrieval systems, without permission in writing from the publisher, except by reviewers, who may quote brief passages in a review.

ISBN 13: 978-1-7323805-2-3

Most characters and events in this book are fictitious. Any similarity to real persons, living or dead, is coincidental and not intended by the author.

All photographs are the property of Shelby L. Syckes unless otherwise credited

Printed in the United States of America

Dedication

For

Stan & Steve

Table of Contents

Foreword 1

Chapter One: Veterans Day - 11 November 1972 4

Chapter Two: Three Months Earlier 8

Chapter Three: The Cave 12

Chapter Four: Peskin's and Pat Bandershot 15

Chapter Five: Noah and Jesse 19

Chapter Six: It's a Killer 24

Chapter Seven: The Night Before 29

Chapter Eight: The Colonel's Funeral 38

Chapter Nine: Key Club 45

Chapter Ten: A Suspect 51

Chapter Eleven: I Didn't Do It 62

Chapter Twelve: The Case is Closed 68

Chapter Thirteen: A Closer Look 74

Chapter Fourteen: Backups 77

Chapter Fifteen: Seeing Things 83

Chapter Sixteen: Puzzle Pieces 92

Chapter Seventeen: Checkup 96

Chapter Eighteen: Jack's Office 104

Chapter Nineteen: Burn Them 111

Chapter Twenty: Clues 122

Chapter Twenty-One: The Report 129
Chapter Twenty-Two: All is Calm 139
Chapter Twenty-Three: Tie Clip 144
Chapter Twenty-Four: Smile 151
Chapter Twenty-Five: Déjà vu 160
Chapter Twenty-Six: The Metric System 167
Chapter Twenty-Seven: Back to the Armory 174
Chapter Twenty-Eight: Up on the Roof 184
Chapter Twenty-Nine: Happy New Year 190
Acknowledgments 195

Foreword

I did not know Shelby Syckes in Allegany High School. I graduated a few years before him but knew his family well. He was the drum major of the band, and I was basically in nothing. His dad was Lu Syckes, who was the music teacher at Allegany, where I struggled for one year as a violinist in the orchestra. Mr. Syckes also owned Uncle Lu's Tastee Freeze in LaVale. Shelby's mom, Stella, operated the Br'er Rabbit Kindergarten in the Dingle, which I attended during my formative years.

It was by way of Facebook a year or so back that Shelby and I became friends and arranged to meet on his next visit to Cumberland. This meeting occurred over a trio of Coney Island wieners. Shelby gave me an autographed copy of his first book, *Slow, Children Playing - On the Way to Band Camp, A Memoir*, which I found to be a most fun read as it pertains to life in Cumberland and its history. In it, Shelby details, in vivid prose, the exploits of a teenage boy as he navigates high school. It contains dozens of stories about many of the people (teachers and others), events (football games, parades, etc.), haunts, and businesses every baby boomer grew up with during the 1960s and 1970s. The local references are too plentiful even to try to list, and all of it reminded me of what a grand time it was growing up in Cumberland during this period. There is also some "gossip." But what's most important is Shelby writes it all down entertainingly and engagingly. I still hopscotch through it whenever I need a smile or a pleasant memory evoked.

I was enjoying my third "with everything" wiener when Shelby informed me of his latest literary work, entitled *Slippery When Wet*. It is much the same yet quite different from his first book. It's a murder mystery set in Cumberland. Some might be surprised and say, "A murder mystery in Cumberland, how unusual?" Not really. There was the 1870 shooting of William Wallace McKaig, Jr. on a busy downtown street. A question of family honor, McKaig had been having an illicit affair with the shooter's sister. And the still unsolved death of Odessa Meister whose bashed body was found buried under a pile of *Life Magazine*s in 1953. I could go on and list several others of more recent vintage, but the bottom line is, murder is no stranger to the Queen City.

Slippery When Wet is a fast-paced and gripping read. Each chapter is like one of those Netflix serials where you can't wait to see the next episode or, in this case, the next page. The time is the early 1970s, and Shelby interweaves his story with Cumberland history like how it was a stop on the Underground Railroad and the Vietnam War's shadow over our generation. The book is filled with numerous local landmarks, people, and businesses, which should ring a bell with many of us. But, even if you've never been to Cumberland, you'll enjoy the adventure and easily relate it to your teenage years.

It starts with a bang. Colonel Bandershot, the commander at our local Maryland National Guard Armory, has been blown to pieces and in front of half the town. Who did it? Was it his beautiful wife, her lover, the sergeant, or someone else? The plot absorbs the reader into a mystery and adventure involving four young people as they follow the leads and track a killer throughout the streets of Cumberland. It is also one of those reads that challenges you to try to guess the culprit. There are clues if you are clever enough to use them. Mix in sex, murder, the local aristocracy, and even some national politics, and you have *Slippery When Wet*. Just make sure you keep both hands on the wheel while reading it. Enjoy.

Albert L. Feldstein
Historian, Author, and Local Denizen

Chapter One
Veterans Day - 11 November 1972

The Appalachian mountain air was so cold that I had my whistle in my mouth to keep it warm. As drum major, I was in front of the Allegany High School band, and we had been standing at attention in near-freezing temperatures for the past twenty minutes. The fall wind sent dry leaves skittering across the parking lot of the Maryland National Guard Armory like waterbugs on a calm pond, but it was too cold to think about water. I was waiting for Dad, the band director, to signal me to start the band playing. He was watching for Colonel Mike Bandershot to make his entrance.

"It's freezing!" said Kris, our first chair flute player, who was standing only feet in front of me. "How much longer do we have to wait for this guy?"

"Forever," said Nora, the flute player beside her. "Bandershot and his big metal toy are why we, and half the city, are here."

"My flute feels like a popsicle," Kris said as her fellow flutists giggled.

"Quiet," I hissed from the side of my mouth, not letting the whistle slip as I looked to my right to see if the colonel had appeared yet.

There it was, the object that had brought us all together today and was the center of everyone's focus. It looked like a giant toad with a white star painted on its side and green straw sticking out of its mouth. Having grown up in a Cold War

Chapter One - Veterans Day - 11 November 1972

world where intercontinental missiles carrying hydrogen bombs could silently descend on us at any time, this World War Two relic looked almost laughable. It was an M4 Sherman tank, and I knew it was one of the linchpin weapons of the Second World War, but to my baby boomer eyes, it just was not that impressive. But, much like Colonel Bandershot, it must have been something special in its day.

According to the morning paper, the Army built almost fifty thousand of them, and now Cumberland was getting one of their own.

"Go!" Dad yelled at me from across the parking lot near the huddling spectators. That's when I saw the little man in his olive-green Army fatigues strutting down the armory's stairs. He walked with purpose, and you could tell he was tightly wired. Everything on him was perfect from his pencil-thin Ronald Colman mustache to his rigidly tied boot laces. You could have cut butter with his pants creases. I heard someone to my left in the platoon of green-fatigued men shout, "Squad, attention," and they all squared up and faced forward. It was march time.

I blew my whistle twice and threw my arms over my head, signaling the band it was time to start. I loved being the guy out front and in charge, but today, all I wanted was to finish this gig and get into a warm building—I swore I could hear ice crystals forming in my ears.

The colonel had reached the bottom step of the staircase before I could start the band, and he was already clambering up the side of the tank as the first few bars of the Army's official song, "The Caissons Go Rolling Along," blared out.

On top of the tank now, the colonel stood as tall as his five-feet-four inches would allow him. His legs were astride, and his hands were on his hips as he scanned the shivering crowd with his chin jutting out like the tank's main gun. It was an impressive sight. Despite the temperature, there were more than two hundred of Cumberland's finest here today cheering and waving the colonel on including Mayor Ed Conklin, the city council, the colonel's beautiful wife, Pat, and a ceremonial contingent from the Freemasons' Shriners auxiliary festooned in red-and-yellow satin pantaloons and topped with fezzes.

The spectators started clapping to the beat of the march, and I saw the colonel reach down and take a microphone from an overweight sergeant. The march ended, and I gave the "parade rest" order to the band just as the heavyset guy returned to his control table and flipped on the amplification system. There was a screech of feedback and then a rustling sound as the colonel's mic came to life.

"Ladies and gentlemen, welcome to what represents the culmination of many years of hard work procuring for our fair city a symbol of our victory over fascism twenty-seven years ago," Colonel Bandershot said to the crowd in his reedy voice as he bobbed his head up and down and smiled more broadly than you would think was possible. "Let us join our voices together in singing 'God Bless America.'" He looked in my direction, and his smile disappeared.

Chapter One - Veterans Day - 11 November 1972

I knew I was being given an order. Not waiting for Dad's approval, I turned back to the band and tweeted my whistle four times. More subtly than the march, the first strains of "God Bless America" sang out over the crowd.

Satisfied that his order had been followed, Colonel Bandershot smiled again, and he bent over to release the locking mechanism on the tank's hatch. He then swung it open and dropped down into the tank commander's seat. As he did, there was a metal clattering sound, and he looked down to see what was making the noise.

My bet was his last conscious thought was an angry one like "What idiot left a grenade in here?"

The tank's turret did a good job of containing the shrapnel from the explosion although a few of the razor-sharp metal shards passed through the colonel's head and fell harmlessly to the ground, some near the feet of a startled drum major. The rest of the concussive force shredded the lower half of Colonel Bandershot. From the waist down, he was nothing but bloody coleslaw.

The music stopped, and a wave of reaction pulsed through the crowd as they felt more than heard the grenade's blast. The loudspeakers thundered then thudded as the microphone, still on, tumbled to the bottom of the tank's interior along with what was left of Colonel Bandershot.

Chapter Two
Three Months Earlier

I'd never had a problem like this before—too much booze. Here I was on my way home from band camp with a trunk filled with six cases of beer and a case of Boone's Farm wine. How did a seventeen-year-old mediocre baritone player leave West Virginia University's Fine Arts Music Camp with all this alcohol?

Well, let's just say I creatively escaped prosecution by convincing the head counselor to let me lock it in the trunk of my car instead of confiscating it and turning me into the camp director. I had planned a big end-of-camp party and collected money from other campers to pay for it, but when I was busted, and the party was called off, I kept the refreshments.

I knew that was a pretty crappy thing to do, given I essentially stole the stuff from my fellow campers, but that wasn't the problem. The problem was, I couldn't take all this booze into my house or leave it in the car. I needed a place to hide it, and I needed that place fast—I would be home in less than an hour.

All that beer and wine was equal to more than a month's salary from my job at my father's Tastee Freez, and there was no way I was going to let our cleaning lady find it in my closet or hide it where some other juvenile delinquent could enjoy it.

Chapter Two - Three Months Earlier

"Hey, the Tastee Freez," I said. I could hide it in the storage area behind the big ice cream cone boxes, and I was only a few miles from there. So, I headed for my dad's second job location, Uncle Lu's Tastee Freez.

Uncle Lu's was doing great; business was up by twenty percent over last year. More business meant more supplies, and wouldn't you know it, as I pulled into the parking lot, there by the back door was the franchise delivery truck. So much for my plan to hide the booze at Uncle Lu's. There was no way I was going to sneak six cases of beer and a case of wine in there while men in overalls wheeled in boxes of pickles and mayonnaise. I parked the car and reassessed my options.

Deep in thought, I was shaken back to reality when the Barracuda started bouncing up and down like a bucking bronco. I instinctively jammed my foot on the brake pedal even though my car was off. I heard laughter and saw my best friend, Tim, and his smiling face as he jumped off the back of my car and leered into the side window. Sandy-haired, lean, and lanky, Tim was eight months short of my age but four inches taller than me. He was no giant; I was just small.

"Jesus H. Christ, Tim! Are you humping my car?"

"Yes, and it was good for me," Tim boasted. "Where have you been? I haven't seen you since the Fourth of July."

"Band camp, remember? I told you I'd be out of town for a few weeks."

Tim laughed. "Oh yeah, so did you get laid?"

Slippery When Wet

Tim never wasted time with niceties. The answer was no, of course, but I'd come closer than I ever had before. I got tagged out at third base.

I shined my fingernails on my shirt. "Absolutely. Sometimes, twice a night. Band chicks are easy."

Before I had to elaborate or, God forbid, tell the truth, I diverted. "Tim, take a look at this." I got out of the car and moved to the back.

I looked around to make sure no adults were within viewing range and popped the trunk of the Barracuda. There lay six stacked cases of Schlitz beer and a cardboard box with twelve bottles of Boone's Farm Strawberry Hill wine stacked side by side and separated by strips of cardboard.

"Holy cow!" Tim exclaimed. "Did you rob a liquor store?"

"No, it's a long story, and I can't waste time telling you. I've got to stash this stuff somewhere fast because I'm scheduled to pick up my mom at Peskin's in half an hour. She never leaves work without buying something, given she spends three-quarters of her salary on clothes, and I can't have this stuff in my trunk when she opens it to put her new Yves Saint Laurent pantsuit in there. Got any ideas?"

Tim scratched his chin as I closed the trunk. "How about the band room? Your dad has the keys, and you could stash it in the instrument closet."

"Are you kidding? If I got caught with one beer on the school grounds, they'd suspend me for a week. Who knows what they'd do if they found me with all of this?"

Chapter Two - Three Months Earlier

"All right, all right. Let me think some more."

"I want it to be someplace I can get to easily but not accessible to others," I added.

"You mean like your crotch?" Tim laughed and bent forward, enjoying his joke.

"You're not helping," I sneered.

"I've got it," Tim said. "The cave. Put it in the cave."

"You mean the one in the cliffs behind the reservoir?"

"Yeah, it's only five minutes from your house, and we could hide it in there, and it's a great place to party."

It wasn't perfect, but it was plausible, and I was out of time, so I told Tim to get his car and follow me to the reservoir.

Chapter Three
The Cave

Cumberland is a sleepy little city that's wedged like a doorstop between Pennsylvania and West Virginia near the thinnest part of the Maryland panhandle. The cave was on the west side of town in an outcropping of cliffs that was part of an Appalachian foothill—just across the highway from my neighborhood.

The cliffs stood high above the Potomac River as it snaked its way south into West Virginia. They were dotted with small caves, but the one Tim had in mind sat just beneath a ledge and was obscured by an overgrowth of brush. You had to go down a zigzagging path and around bushes before you even saw the entrance. It was broader and deeper than any of the other caves and a favorite playground for Tim and me on lazy summer afternoons. Now we used it as a drinking spot.

I parked my car a few blocks past the reservoir on a dead-end street overlooking the Maryland National Guard Armory and waited. Tim didn't show up for another fifteen minutes. He pulled up behind me and got out of his Opel station wagon carrying a large half-eaten dip-top ice cream cone.

"What took you so long? I've only got fifteen minutes before I pick up Mom."

"Hey, man, I had to get an ice cream cone. That's what I was doing at your dad's store. You know he sells ice cream there, don't you?" Tim wiped his mouth on his sleeve.

Chapter Three - The Cave

"Can you carry four cases?" I asked. "I can handle the other two and the box of wine."

"Sure, but we aren't going to be able to carry all of those into the cave at once. There is no way we'll make it down that path with that much stuff in our arms," Tim said.

"Right, but I don't want to make more than one trip from here to the cliffs. We are way too exposed," I said while lifting cases of beer one at a time and stacking them on Tim's open arms. He had carefully placed his ice cream cone on the curb hoping it would wait for him to return.

As Tim trudged off towards the woods at the end of the street, I stacked the last two cases on top of the wine box and lifted them all at once. They were heavier than I expected, and the top case slipped off and crashed to the pavement below. I heard a hissing sound and then saw a shaft of foam bubble up from under the bottom six-pack. One of the beer cans had burst from the impact and was emptying its contents on the road faster than a racehorse relieves himself.

I grabbed the injured can and clamped my lips around the punctured opening.

It didn't take long for the pressure to equalize, and the leaking stopped. I put the beer in the wine box with the punctured end up, planning to return to it later. After rebalancing the cases on the wine box, I was off to find Tim.

A footpath behind the armory led into a wood of deciduous trees thick with summer leaves that hugged me with darkness. I found Tim on the ledge over the cave swinging on a knotted rope that we had tied to an overhead branch years ago. It was positioned just right so we could swing on it in an arching angle to another ledge about ten yards away—if you were going fast enough and hung on tightly. If you didn't, you would drop twenty feet into a forest of rhododendrons.

He was enjoying a beer as he clutched the rope with his free hand and pirouetted in small circles.

"Hey, that's my beer your drinking!" I yelled as I came up behind him and carefully rested my boxes on the ground.

"Yeah, and I know where you're going to hide it, so do you really want to piss me off? Besides, this was my idea."

"Listen, I have to get going. Can you stash this stuff in the cave for me? I'll give you the rest of that six-pack you started if you do."

"No problem. I'll catch up with you tomorrow," Tim said while holding his beer out as he continued to spin like a whirling dervish.

"Thanks." I grabbed the injured beer from the wine box and ran back to my car. Sucking it dry, I set it down next to Tim's ice cream cone, now reduced by the sun to a runny cream puddle.

"Tim will do a good job hiding the booze," I said to myself as I popped a stick of Juicy Fruit gum into my mouth to hide any lingering traces of beer.

We'd been friends for ten years and been through a lot together. What I didn't know then was that our biggest adventure was just ahead of us.

Chapter Four
Peskin's and Pat Bandershot

I bounded up the back stairs of Peskin's Department Store only to be stopped at the mezzanine by the owner, Mort Peskin.

"Slow down, cowboy! I'm running a business here not a rodeo."

"Sorry, Mr. Peskin. I'm here to pick up Mom."

"I hear you, but slow down, and on behalf of the Downtown Cumberland Businessmen's Association, thank you."

Mort Peskin was a big man with a big heart, but that heart was designed to sell. Maybe you'd heard the adage about the excellent salesman who could sell ice to Eskimos. Well, Mort could sell them a Frigidaire to keep it cold.

Mom had been working for Peskin's since 1966 when she sold her kindergarten business, and she loved it. If ever anyone was suited for a job, Mom was tailor-made for this one. She adored women's fashions, so as the manager of the women's fashion floor of one of Cumberland's high-end department stores, she was in hog heaven.

It was Saturday, so that meant Mom would be getting off work at five o'clock, and it was my job to get her home in time to change for an evening at the Cumberland Country Club. Dad was already there, having played golf all day, and would change clothes in the locker room for their evening together.

I continued up the stairs, but at a more respectable pace, and found Maxine, the store's aging seamstress, putting on her coat. Before I could ask, Maxine said, "She's in the fitting room with that shiksa Army bitch."

I knew at once who Maxine meant: Pat Bandershot, the wife of the Maryland National Guard Armory's commander. Mrs. Bandershot was a Cumberland native who turned her beauty pageant looks into a convenient marriage to the son of the wealthiest man in town.

Maxine brushed past me as she waddled towards the stairs. I went to find Mom, and as I passed her desk, I grabbed a handful of M&Ms from the jarful of sweets she always had handy. I couldn't pass up M&Ms.

High-ceilinged and oval-shaped, Peskin's fashion floor looked like an overly decorated wedding cake with colorfully clothed mannequins playing the part of the bride and groom. The majority of the overhead lights were off because it was fifteen minutes after closing time, but the recessed lights in the display areas made it safe to navigate.

I heard voices coming from the fitting room on the far side, and I didn't have to get too close to know someone was upset.

"Stella, this rag is not me. Don't you have anything more fashion-forward and in a size four?"

Chapter Four - Peskin's and Pat Bandershot

"Pat, you're wearing a copy of the Halston Liza Minnelli wore to the Oscars, and it's a size six. If I put you in a four, you won't be able to breathe."

"Well, it will clash with the patent leather Gucci pumps Mort just ordered for me, so I don't want it. Sorry, Stella, but I'll have to look for something when I'm in DC with Mike next week."

There was some fumbling, and then the door to the fitting room opened. Out pranced Pat Bandershot in a slip that barely covered her slim and shapely pantyhosed legs.

She still looked damned good for a woman thirty years my senior.

Mrs. Bandershot flew by me and went straight to the fitting room on the other side of the store. Mom was carrying at least ten outfits, and when she saw me, she nodded at the chair near the wall indicating I might as well sit down. It was going to be a while.

Mom put the clothes on a settee and began to return them to their proper locations in the banks of recessed closets along the curved walls. It was ten minutes before Mrs. Bandershot exited the fitting room, fully dressed this time and carrying a bra.

"And I want to return this. It's just too tight." She tossed the bra onto the cashier's desk and glided to the elevator.

As she pushed the down button, Mom said, "Pat, you'll have to use the back stairs. Ethel the elevator operator left at five."

Looking as if she'd been asked to clean the toilets, Mrs. Bandershot followed Mom to the stairs without saying a word.

I was finishing my M&Ms and inspecting the bra on the cashier's desk when Mom returned. It was a size thirty-eight D-cup.

"Put that down; it's dirty enough already. I can't believe she had the nerve to return an item she wore for a week." Mom took the bra from my hand and looked at it carefully. "Here, look here, there are sweat stains on the straps."

I didn't look, knowing Mom was wound tight, and I didn't want to push her release button accidentally.

"It's a total write-off, and that money impacts my commission," Mom said while still looking at the bra. "It's not the first time she's done this. Last February, she returned a two-hundred-dollar evening dress claiming she hadn't worn it. Christ, I saw her in it at the country club the night before. That's moxie."

"Is she always so nasty?" I asked.

"Only when she's been drinking, and she smells like a distillery today. I don't understand it. Pat used to be such a sweet girl. I sang with her in the Episcopal choir before she was married, but I don't think that's worked out as well as she hoped." Mom's face tightened, and her eyes darted down. There was a long pause, and then she said, "Forget that, I've said too much," and she immediately changed the subject. "How was band camp?"

Chapter Five
Noah and Jesse

August gave way to September, and before I knew it, October was starting. Tim's choice of the cave as a hiding place was a good one. At first, we regularly visited there and enjoyed a beer or three and had buzzed through more than half of our stash, but it had been a few weeks since we'd been back due to our busy band season. One downside of the cave was no refrigeration, so we had to take some ice and wait for the cans to cool down before partying. We didn't bother with the wine. I'd had a very bad Boone's Farm experience my junior year, and I did not intend to repeat it.

It was Thursday afternoon, and I was lounging on my bed listening to my *Blood, Sweat & Tears* eight-track tape when the phone rang. I reached over, pulled the tape box out of the machine, and then lifted the receiver. "Hello."

"Listen, I've got you a date for Saturday night, but we have to go to the Noah Coffeehouse," Tim announced without introduction.

"Who's the date?"

"You'll love her. She has a great personality and makes her own clothes," Tim joked. "Nah, listen, it's Katie's relative from out of town, and she's hot. Well, at least she's hot enough for you."

"Katie Bandershot?" I asked.

"Yeah, I've been hitting on her in band for weeks, and I finally got her to go out with me, but she can't go alone, and her mom will only let her go to the coffeehouse in the basement of your church. Oh, and this weekend, her cousin Joni from Massachusetts is in town, so all the pieces are in place except the cousin's date, and you're the date."

"Sure, but you have to drive; I'm not playing chauffeur."

"Okay, I'll pick you up at eight. Be ready and try to look good," Tim finished.

"Bite me," I said and hung up.

Katie Bandershot was one of Allegany's talented twirlers. She was blonde and petite with a full figure, having inherited her mother's proportions. She reminded me of *I Dream of Jeannie*'s Barbara Eden. I knew this was Tim's big chance, so I had to help. Luckily for me, it turned out her cousin Joni was pretty, too. Maybe too pretty, but she tolerated me, so there was hope. Joni was Katie's bookend, only with brassy brown hair and a Boston accent.

The Noah Coffeehouse had been up and running at my church for three years, and I'd stopped going to it about a year ago because I couldn't bring beer. It was in the basement of the parish hall, a general-purpose building attached to the church. The ceilings were low, and candles were the only lighting for the small tables where kids crowded together. Joni was looking good, and after an hour, I thought it would be nice if we could move our party to a more private location, like the cave, where we could treat the girls to a beer.

Chapter Five - Noah and Jesse

I nudged Tim and whispered, "Come out in the hall with me. I have an idea."

We feigned a need to visit the bathroom and left the table, but when we got to the hallway, I saw Allan, the coffeehouse manager, standing there. I didn't want him overhearing Tim and me planning a beer party.

"Follow me," I said to Tim and turned to go through what looked like a broom closet door. But it wasn't a closet; it was the entrance to the underground tunnels that crisscrossed beneath the church's foundation. They were the only thing remaining from the days when Fort Cumberland stood on this site during the French and Indian War. Initially used by the military to shuttle troops without having to exit the fort, the tunnels also served as a hiding place for slaves traveling on the Underground Railroad after the church was built. Nowadays, the tunnels were used for storage and a way for the minister and acolytes to get to the altar area without going through the church. Having been an acolyte for years, I'd spent a lot of time in the tunnels.

I pulled the string below a naked light bulb, and it bathed the front of the tunnel in harsh white light. "Listen, how about we talk the girls into going up to the cave for a beer? It might relax them a bit," I suggested to Tim.

"I don't know. Katie's mom was really clear about only going to the coffeehouse," Tim cautioned.

"Yeah, I know, but if they are willing to go, aren't you?"

"Sure, I am—"

"You boys have some beer in a cave?" a resonant voice asked from out of the dark end of the tunnel.

I saw the pulsing tip of his cigarette before anything else. It was alive and in rhythm with his breathing. His face appeared through a cloud of smoke. Luckily for us, it was a kind face.

"It's cool. I'm cool. Don't be shitting your pants over little old me. I'm Jesse Preslor. You boys don't remember me, do you?" He held out his right hand in Tim's direction.

Tim shook it as I tried to look calm. One of the largest black men I'd ever seen came into full view.

"Sorry, ah I, ah, don't," Tim stuttered.

Jesse smiled broadly. "You're one of Doc Lewis's kids. My mom used to clean house for you a few years back. Sometimes, I'd come with her when she couldn't get a sitter. I remember playing with you and your brothers." He turned, and my hand disappeared into his. "And you're the band director's son, aren't you? I played trombone in the band and graduated in seventy. I guess I look a little different; I'm four inches taller and fifty pounds heavier now."

"Yeah, that's me," I said, as the smell of his cigarette told me it was a joint. "What are you doing in the tunnel in the dark?"

"The Reverend Cooper doesn't believe weed is part of the Apostles' Creed, so I do my smoking in here. I help out my father at the church; he's the sexton. Want some?" Jesse said as he pushed his reefer in my direction.

Chapter Five - Noah and Jesse

"No thanks. As you heard, we've got some beer waiting for us."

"Yeah, sounds good. You need any help with that?" Jesse asked.

"Do you like Boone's Farm wine? We've got a case of it, and we can't stand it."

I saw a gleam of an idea in Jesse's sharp brown eyes. "Nah, that is some powerful lousy shit, but maybe I can take it off your hands. I run a little business on the side selling nickel bags of weed, and offering a free bottle of wine with every purchase might give me an edge in the market. You know, differentiate my product from the ten other dope dealers in town. We're all selling the same ditch weed, but maybe I can get more business if my ditch weed comes with shitty wine." Jesse laughed aloud. "I'm new to the business; I've only been back in Cumberland for three months."

I looked at Tim, and he nodded. "Okay, Jesse, let us go talk to our dates and see if they want to party at the cave. If they say yes, you can join us. If they say no, after we take them home, we will meet you for a boys' only night."

After some whispered explanations and prompting, the girls agreed to go, so I went back to the tunnel and told Jesse to meet us at the armory in an hour because we had to stop to get some ice to cool down the beer first.

"You don't need any stinking ice," Jesse said. "Forget it and head straight there."

Chapter Six
It's a Killer

Jesse didn't look as big standing in the parking lot of the armory as he did in the tunnel, but he was still big. He made the high-pressure tank he was holding look like a toy. The tank reminded me of the ones you would hook up to your outdoor barbecue grill. I had no clue why he had it.

Jesse was not the typical early 1970s black guy. There was no oversized Afro hairstyle or brightly colored dashiki caftan. Jesse was wearing jeans and a flannel shirt, and his hairstyle was high and tight. He looked like Cassius Clay before he became Muhammad Ali.

"What's that?" Joni asked Jesse as she bounded out of the car and ran over to him. I knew at once I was coming in second in the popularity contest tonight.

"You'll see," Jesse said, looking down from his six-foot-four vantage point at Joni's five-foot-two gaze.

I got out of the car with the others and grabbed an oversized flashlight from the glovebox. "This way." I pointed to the woods behind the armory.

"You going onto the armory's property?" Jesse asked ominously.

"Nope, to the cliffs behind it. That's where the cave is."

"Good, I guess I should have told you I'm a member of the Maryland National Guard."

We all stopped walking and turned to look back at Jesse.

Chapter Six - It's a Killer

"It's cool. Don't worry. I'm certainly not a narc. Remember, you just caught me smoking dope in the church's basement."

"That explains your haircut," Tim said.

"Yeah, I got drafted right out of high school and trained with the Army's Quartermasters Corps. After six months at Fort Lee, they shipped me off to Saigon where I spent ten months washing dishes. I guess it beat chasing Charlie in the bush."

"Wow, Vietnam," both Joni and Katie gushed.

I looked at Tim, and he shook his head. Not only were we physically smaller than Jesse, our résumés could not compete either.

Jesse lifted the pressurized tank and curled it like a weightlifter. "After that, I took a few months off and bummed around, but I've got my shit in a pile now and plan to use Uncle Sam's money to pay for my education. I just started classes out at the community college."

"Aren't you taking a bit of a risk selling weed as a member of the National Guard?" I asked.

"I guess, but my best customers are my fellow guardsmen."

"You better be nice to me or I'll tell my daddy," Katie warned him.

"What are you talking about?" Jesse asked.

"Well, I guess we should have told you that Miss Bandershot here is your commanding officer's daughter," I said.

Jesse snapped to attention and saluted Katie. Everyone laughed, and both girls walked with him as we all pushed into the woods.

I moved the pine tree branches off the one remaining case of Schlitz and grabbed a six-pack. It was room, or should I say cave, temperature—not too good for drinking.

"Give me that," said Jesse, taking the six-pack and spreading it open on the ground like a fan and not detaching the cans from the plastic rings. He moved the high-pressure tank next to them and picked up the black rubber hose attached to its top. The hose had a specialized nozzle at its end and a release valve.

"What's that?" Tim asked.

"Freon," Jesse said, as he opened the valve and pointed the hissing end of the hose at the beers. The cans disappeared in a cloud of dirt, but thirty seconds later, they had an icy coating and were looking frosty.

"We use it at the church to top off the air conditioner. There you go. They should be drinkable now, but be careful, your skin will stick to the icy cans," said our very own Mr. Freeze.

We settled in for a cozy party, and I made a point of talking with Joni in the hope of kindling some kind of a relationship.

Jesse bought the case of Boone's Farm from me for eight dollars, and he gave me an extra dollar to cover the cost of his beer. The girls shared a Schlitz. After an hour, they made it clear they needed to be home soon, so we gathered up our trash and left the cave.

Chapter Six - It's a Killer

Jesse, having drunk a six-pack on his own, was no longer concerned about trespassing on armory property as we made our way back to the cars.

"Let me show you where I play soldier," he said, reaching into his pants pocket and removing a key ring. "The sergeant won't mind since we've got Colonel Bandershot's little girl with us. What's he going to do anyway?"

We walked up a broad flight of stairs, and he used a key to unlock the front door of the armory. Before us was a low-ceilinged entry hall that led to a full-sized gymnasium equipped with a basketball court and bleachers, but they were stowed away that night, so the gym floor was wide-open. The exit sign's green glow mixed with the moonlight to give the space an otherworld appearance.

"What do you do in here?" Joni asked.

"Drill, and I don't mean like a dentist," Jesse said.

Tim made a throwing motion with his arm. "This would be a great place to throw a Frisbee."

"Frisbees! You guys into throwing Frisbees?" Jesse asked.

I crossed myself. "Does the pope shit in the woods? Tim, you've got a couple in the car, don't you?"

"Always," Tim said, and I left to get them.

I came back with two plastic disks, and we spent the next hour sailing them around the armory's drill area without a care in the world. Although we kept the lights off to avoid drawing attention, Katie went into her father's office and brought out his portable record player and some of his vast record collection. We got them spinning, and even though the music was a bit dated, the Big Band sound amplified our fun. We also danced a little, but none of us really knew how to jitterbug. The girls forgot about their curfew.

Tim and I thought we were good Frisbee throwers, but Jesse was masterful. Even in the low light, he could topple a beer can sitting on a tabletop from across the room. Sometimes, it took him more than one try, but Tim and I couldn't even hit the table.

"Where did you learn how to throw so well?"

Jesse got a smirk on his face. "When we weren't washing dishes, it was pretty boring in Vietnam. Frisbees were scarce, so my buddies and I found creative substitutes. We learned to throw pie tins, pot tops, and even garbage can lids: anything disk-shaped became one of our toys."

Jesse demonstrated for us as we left the armory by grabbing the lid of a trash can, and with a powerful right arm motion, he sent it sailing across the parking lot. It smoothly landed and slid into a sewer drain like a hockey puck scoring a hat trick.

"Wow!" I said.

Jesse smiled and winked. "That's my overhand throw; it's a killer."

Chapter Seven
The Night Before

After our fun at the armory with Jesse, Tim and I started partying with him regularly. Although a little older than us, he was a kid at heart and hadn't reconnected with his old friends since he'd been back. Jesse came to our football games and joined us afterward to throw Frisbees and drink beer. Tim locked down Katie as his steady girlfriend, which made him a very happy boy. I was still flying solo as the warm weather of October downshifted to a cold November. By Friday the tenth, the freezing temperature forced the band to practice inside.

There wasn't a football game that night, so Jesse asked us over to his house. Tim and I got to Jesse's at seven o'clock, and his father let us in, but Jesse wasn't home from the armory yet. He was tied up prepping for Colonel Bandershot's tank ceremony scheduled for the next morning.

Jesse's dad was a stocky fifty-five-year-old who looked seventy. His white curls had abandoned his head, and his shoulders sagged as if weights were attached to his arms. According to Jesse, he had been an algebra teacher at a segregated high school, but when the schools were integrated, he lost his job and now worked at my church.

It was the fall of 1955 when Cumberland implemented the Supreme Court ruling of Brown vs. the Board of Education in a shining example of our city's egalitarian principles at

Slippery When Wet

work. That's how I had heard it, but Jesse shared a different perspective.

Integration was a one-way street. The city closed the black schools, and their students all went to the white ones, but their teachers were not invited to follow them. That meant the faculty and staff of the black schools found themselves unemployed, and it stayed that way for most of them.

Jesse's father's situation was a good example. Even though he had a bachelor's degree in mathematics and a master's in education, the only job he could get in Cumberland was as sexton of the Emmanuel Episcopal Church. Sexton is a fancy name for janitor and gravedigger.

"Come on in and sit down. I'll get you a Coke." Jesse's dad pointed to the small living room crowded with a sofa and armchair.

The house was modest even by Cumberland standards, and there was no sign of a woman's housekeeping touch. Jesse's mother had died five years earlier. A pile of newspapers sat next to a cluttered desk, and on the wall above the television set were two framed diplomas flanked by photos of Martin Luther King, Jr. and J.F.K.

Jesse's dad handed us a glass with ice and popped the tops of two small green Coke bottles. "Jesse tells me he met you boys in the tunnel at the church."

"Yes, sir," Tim said.

"Did he tell you how our family got started in that tunnel?"

Chapter Seven - The Night Before

Tim looked at me quizzically and got a mirror image. "No, sir. How can a tunnel start a family?"

"His great-grandfather was born in there a few months after his mother found her way to freedom. She escaped slavery in North Carolina," Jesse's dad said with a serious yet proud voice. "You know the Emmanuel parish was a stop on the Underground Railroad? Please tell me they teach you boys about the Underground Railroad in school."

"Yes, sir," Tim said. "It was a network of abolitionist and like-minded southerners who helped slaves travel north to freedom."

Jesse's dad's face turned stern. "There were no like-minded southerners. Those people were hell-bent on maintaining their way of life, and that meant doing whatever it took to keep their workers in chains, and for the last hundred years, they've continued to keep the black man down."

Jesse's dad's passion pressurized the room. Tim sank into the couch, and I cooled my lips with a sip of Coke.

"Sorry, boys, I know I can be a little intense when discussing this, but it's personal to me. You see, if it hadn't been for the courage of sixteen-year-old Sally Preslor, I wouldn't be here today, and neither would Jesse. She was something special. It was 1857 when she escaped from down south and made her way over three hundred miles to Cumberland."

"That's amazing," I said.

Mr. Preslor nodded. "Darn right. Especially when you consider the law of the land back then did not recognize her as a human being. She was property and, without a legal bill of sale, stolen property."

Mr. Preslor stopped and took a drink from his tumbler of whiskey. "It was a very risky gamble.

"Some men made their living hunting down runaway slaves like Sally and returning them to their owners for a handsome price. A healthy young woman like her was considered good breeding stock and would have been worth maybe ten thousand dollars in today's money. Why, if she'd been caught and returned to her master, who knows what he would have done to her. How those people called themselves Christian is beyond me," Jesse's dad's voice trailed off, and his focus shifted to the floor. "Sorry again, I didn't mean to preach."

"What happened to your great-grandfather Preslor, Sally's husband?" Tim asked.

"There was no husband, and there were no last names. Preslor was the plantation owner's name, and back then, Sally was what they called a house nigger." Jesse's dad made a popping sound after saying that last word as if he was spitting a seed on the floor.

"Oh, she had a lover and might have married him, but she was also subject to the will of her master and told me when I was a child she often had to do his bidding when he needed his bed warmed. So, when she realized she was pregnant, she couldn't be sure who the father was, but it didn't matter to her. What mattered was she didn't want her child to be born a slave, and because of her persistence, he wasn't."

Chapter Seven - The Night Before

"How did she end up in the church tunnel?" I asked.

Mr. Preslor rubbed his callused palms together and nodded his head. "Well, boys, what happened was as close to a miracle as you can get. It took Sally over a month to make her way to Cumberland. She knew she was close to the Mason-Dixon Line when she found herself hiding in a manure dump below the mule stables of the C&O Canal near old Shanty Town. That's where Footers Dry Cleaners is today. Back then, the canal came all the way into Cumberland and had a big port facility across Wills Creek from the church. The Underground Railroad operator who got Sally that far told her to stay there until contacted by another operator. It was a miserable time, and she had to lie down in the muck during the day to avoid being seen."

Jesse's dad's eyes tightened, and his voice slowed. "A stable boy would bring her food, but it was hard to eat it while knee-deep in mule dung. The boy turned out to be the operator Sally was waiting for. After two days, he told her she was to listen that night for a bell to toll three times. She was then to make her way to the church and ask for the station master.

"Sally heard the bells and started to get up out of the mire when two drunks above her started to relieve themselves of their last beer." Mr. Preslor laughed and took another drink. "It only took a few minutes for them to move on, but Sally was sure she was late for her rendezvous. It was raining hard when Sally crawled from her hiding spot and started running along the bank of the creek. She knew where the church was and could see the dark-stoned steeple but wasn't sure where it was safe to cross. The creek was high from the spring thaw, and I'm sure she was scared to death of that water, but she waded in anyway and started to walk along the bottom determined to keep her head above it."

There was a soft crash, and a rolling sound as Tim accidentally bumped his empty Coke bottle while reaching for his glass. "Sorry, Mr. Preslor."

"Don't worry, boy; it isn't the first bottle to hit my floor. Sally made it to the other side and was climbing up the muddy banks when her shoe slipped on a wet rock, and she tumbled backward into the rushing creek. Her terror was still on her face when she told me this story, and I can understand why. When she hit that cold water, it filled her mouth, choking off her cry for help. Sally slipped below the waterline."

"The good Lord must have been watching over her for that's when a strong hand grabbed her and lifted Sally onto the creek bank. As her vision cleared, she saw the warm smiling face of the Reverend Buel of Emmanuel Parish. He had rung the bell, and when no one arrived, he went to investigate. Seeing Sally fall, he jumped into the creek to save her despite wearing his full-length vestments."

I heard myself gasp.

Jesse's dad smiled and rocked back into his armchair. "Yes, sir, that's how it happened. She told me that story herself forty-five years ago, not long before she passed. She loved telling it, and she always finished it the same way—with what Reverend Buel said to her as he pulled her out of that creek and welcomed her into the protective arms of the church and freedom."

Chapter Seven - The Night Before

Jesse took over the narrative. "Reverend Buel told Sally 'You need to take care, girl. The rocks are slippery. They're slippery when wet.' Dad, are you boring my new friends with that fairy tale about Great-Great-Grandmother Sally?"

"It is not a fairy tale, it's the God's honest truth, and you should be proud of it!" boomed Mr. Preslor.

Jesse had come in sometime during the telling, and when I turned to look at him, I saw he was in uniform.

"Atten-hut," I ordered.

"At ease," Jesse said.

"But why did she have her baby in the tunnel under the church?" Tim asked.

Jesse's dad laughed, and the crow's-feet in the corner of his eyes shimmered. "Oh, right. That was the original point of the story, wasn't it? Well, things were heating up back then. Have you heard of the Dred Scott case?"

I looked at Tim.

"Was that when the Supreme Court ruled colored people weren't citizens?"

"That's right. No one was on the black man's side back then, and on top of that, the State of Maryland was giving slave catchers free rein in the state. It just wasn't safe for Sally to continue her trip north, so she hid in the tunnels."

Jesse's dad set his empty tumbler on the coffee table. "It wasn't long before her condition made travel impossible, so the Reverend and Mrs. Buel took care of her making sure she had a safe place to have her baby even though it was on a dirt floor underneath the church. I like to think of it as a nativity scene."

"That's real American history," Tim said.

Jesse interrupted. "Dad would like you to think it is. The reality is, Sally traded being a slave on a plantation for being a slave at the Emmanuel Episcopal Church, and her family has been in bondage at that place ever since."

Jesse's father was standing now, and his smile was gone. "Boy, you have no right to denigrate the hard work of your grandparents. They made the best of their situation."

I kept quiet not wanting to get between a father and son arguing family history.

"How about we hit the road and find a place to throw the Frisbees," Tim interjected, trying to save us.

"Good idea. My whole day has been crap, and I could use a little exercise," Jesse said as he turned towards the staircase. "Bandershot is obsessed with this tank ceremony."

Corporal Preslor went upstairs to change, and Tim and I thanked Mr. Preslor for the Cokes and the history lesson.

As Jesse drove us to play Frisbee, he continued to complain about work. "Sergeant Inversol has had it with Bandershot. The old man jumped all over him in front of the other troops for not rewashing the tank after the rain. You'd think that thing was made of gold, not rolled homogeneous armor. I'm telling you Inversol's pissed. I was outside his office and heard him saying something on the phone about teaching Bandershot a

Chapter Seven - The Night Before

lesson. I'm not sure that's possible. The colonel's head is so full of shit there isn't any room for learning."

Jesse's face glowed ghoulishly from the dashboard's lights. "It was still going on when I left. I saw Inversol opening up the tank with someone else. They were probably making sure it was nice and clean on the inside."

We pulled into the armory's parking lot, and I asked, "Jesse, are you sure you want to use the armory tonight? You've been here all day."

Jesse slammed the door of his VW microbus. "Sure, I don't hate the building, I hate Bandershot."

"Is that the tank?" Tim asked as he pointed to a dark tented mass just left of the main entrance.

"Yeah, that's it, the colonel's baby. It looks like Inversol has covered it up to protect it from the morning dew. I don't get it; it's nothing but a hunk of rusting metal."

"Didn't Bandershot ride one of those up the beach on D-Day or something? He's like some big World War Two hero, isn't he?" I asked.

"Well, I thought so, but when I talked to Inversol about it, he just laughed and said the colonel spent more time behind a bush than in a tank. To tell you the truth, I don't give a damn; I only show up here to keep getting taxpayer money to pay for college." Jesse pulled open the front door. "Let's throw some disks."

Chapter Eight
The Colonel's Funeral

The casket was not open at Colonel Bandershot's funeral; the mortician couldn't sew enough of him back together to make him presentable. The service was at the Episcopal church, and I got tapped to be the crucifer. That meant I had to wear a man-dress and stand by the casket holding a six-foot pole with a cross on top. I also had to be there an hour in advance to help with setup.

As sexton, Mr. Preslor was there, and Jesse was helping too. We hauled the three-piece catafalque from the tunnel to the front of the church just below the steps of the altar. The ancient wooden casket stand was scarred from years of handling.

"I wish they'd use one of those wheeled coffin rollers they've got at the funeral home. This thing weighs a ton," Jesse said as we used a dolly to bump our burden up the stairs.

Mr. Preslor was manhandling the smaller center section. "I hear that. But there's only one way to do things at Emmanuel, and that's the old way. I've been dragging this sorry piece of wood out of the tunnel for every funeral for the last fifteen years except when they cremate the bodies. Then I just set the ash jug on a plant stand."

"Jesse, what's been going on up at the armory? Have they finished the investigation?" I asked.

"They're close. They grilled the other guardsman and me for over an hour. The guys got to leave, but I've been up there

Chapter Eight - The Colonel's Funeral

all week helping them push paper because I'm Inversol's assistant. It's not just us, though, lots of people have been in and out of there. The Army brought in a JAG major who's the boss of everything."

I tugged on Jesse's sleeve. "What's a JAG?"

"Sorry, Judge Advocate General. That's what the military calls their lawyers. He's got jurisdiction over the city police since the crime was committed on a military installation."

"Oh, the police are involved, let me tell you," Mr. Preslor added. "I work nights sometimes down at the station cleaning up things, and they have been burning the midnight oil on this one. I heard that the Army determined the grenade came from the armory's supplies."

"Yeah, I heard that, too," said Jesse, "and it's put the spotlight on Sergeant Inversol. He was the only one I know of who had access to the ordnance bunker under the armory. That thing is buried twenty feet down, and the only way to get to it is through the basement." As we lifted the last piece of the catafalque from the dolly, Jesse directed, "Okay, set your end of this thing down right in front of the first row of pews."

Relieved of my burden, I sat down on a pew. "An Army officer interviewed me, and it was a big nothing. But then, I didn't have anything to tell him other than I heard the explosion and damn near got hit by a piece of shrapnel."

"I'll give them this," Jesse said. "They moved fast to control the scene of the crime. Minutes after the grenade exploded, the police chief ordered everyone into the armory, and by the time the fire department arrived, he'd checked them all for injuries. Luckily, there weren't any: lots of ringing ears, but no bleeding."

"Yeah, my hearing still isn't right," I added. "While I was waiting around, I saw the firefighters hosing down the tank, and police were stringing black-and-yellow crime scene tape everywhere. I even saw the mayor's wife passing a bottle of valium around to her friends."

Jesse went back to the dolly and began to wheel it towards the stairs. "They separated Katie and Mrs. Bandershot from all the others in the colonel's office. Katie was distraught. Tim told me he tried to get in to talk to her, but the police wouldn't let him."

"Before I left, the police chief told me not to discuss the murder with anyone," I said.

"Ha!" Mr. Preslor laughed. "Nobody's followed that order; the murder is topic number one of every conversation everywhere. I've heard no fewer than five theories of the case. Most think it was an inside job given the murder weapon was a grenade, but my mailman thinks it was suicide."

"That's a pretty shitty way to kill yourself, you know. Grenades hurt," I joked. Both Jesse and his father chuckled. "Listen, I've got to go put on my crucifer outfit."

I heard the rear door of the church open, and two men in dark suits wheeled the coffin in. I left to change. After putting on my white nightshirt-like outfit, I took the tunnel to the little room just off the altar. I couldn't help but think about

Chapter Eight - The Colonel's Funeral

Sally as I walked along the narrow dirt path and envisioned her giving birth there. After polishing the gold-plated crucifix atop a wooden staff beautifully aged from years of handling, I reentered the church. By then, mourners littered the pews, and a small contingent of armory personnel mingled near the back waiting for orders.

The flag-draped casket dominated the scene, held gently three feet above the floor by the catafalque. Reverend Cooper whispered and nodded to Mrs. Bandershot in the first pew. Her look was distant, and her eyes were unfocused. Katie sat beside them, and Tim sat next to her. They both busied themselves greeting well-wishers who felt obliged to say something.

I stepped down the stairs to the casket and took my place to the right. Reverend Cooper stood and moved in front of the first pew just as Sergeant Inversol called his men to attention and started them marching down the center aisle. The organ burst forth with the opening chords of "Onward Christian Soldiers," and everyone rose to sing. Reaching the front of the church, the soldiers stood at attention until the music stopped. Then they took their seats.

Sergeant Inversol seemed a bit confused and was last to sit behind his men. As he did, he tripped on the prayer kneeler left down by a previous believer and fell forward, saved only by his girth. Wedged between pew back and pew seat, he squirmed helplessly until two of his men freed him.

The funeral service was like all funeral services: dead. Everyone mouthed the words from the *Book of Common Prayer*, but no one absorbed any meaning. It ended with a mumble: "Amen."

I was able to talk to Katie and Tim after the service while refreshments were served next door in the parish house. "How are you doing?" I asked Katie softly as I squeezed her hand.

"Thanks, I'm doing okay, but I'm tired of answering that question."

"That fat sergeant made a graceful entrance, didn't he?" I added, snickering.

"Leave Jack alone," Katie said with more force than I expected. "He's got bigger problems than I do."

"Sorry, Katie, I didn't know you and that sergeant were friends. It's just that I've seen him on the floor before. Like Tim's father, he plays poker with my dad, and there have been a few nights when he has had trouble getting out the door." I tilted my hand up like I was drinking from a bottle.

Tim nodded. "The man has no bottom where booze is concerned. I saw him in the courtyard behind the church just a few minutes ago sipping from a pint of Jack Daniel's. He was talking with some guy who could have been the singer James Taylor's twin brother."

Katie stamped her foot. "I know, but Jack was very badly injured during the war, and his medication does not keep the pain away for long. Dad used to give him hell about it all the time." Katie looked down at the floor as if saying the word dad added weight to her neck. "You've got to save me from my mom."

"What do you mean?" Tim asked.

Chapter Eight - The Colonel's Funeral

"She's driving me nuts. That thousand-mile stare of hers is all an act. At home, all she does is drink, scream on the phone, and bitch at me. She's talking about selling everything and moving. I don't want to move," Katie said as her voice became a whisper, and her head sank again.

Tim put his arm around her just as Mrs. Bandershot appeared with cousin Joni. "Katherine, straighten up and mingle with our guests. Take Joni with you. These people are here to honor your father, and it's our job to make them feel welcome."

Tim swung his arm off Katie faster than you'd drop a hot rock as we spread out, forced back by Pat Bandershot's gaze.

"Yes, Mother," Katie said.

Reassuming her bereaved demeanor, Mrs. Bandershot turned to engage the crowd. It was time to accept more sad smiles from her friends.

"Save me, please," Katie pleaded as she followed.

I heard Tim whisper to her, "Don't worry; I'll pick you up at eight. Listen for a tap on your window."

Katie nodded and disappeared into the tea-sipping mourners.

I looked at Tim. He tilted his head and nodded towards the door. "Agree," I said, glancing down at my crucifer's outfit. "Let me get out of this wedding gown, and I'll meet you out front."

The acolyte's dressing room was on the top floor of the parish house, and as I was pulling my costume off, I heard men arguing. The voices were coming from the window that overlooked the courtyard. I looked out and saw Sergeant Inversol, but I couldn't see who he was with. The window pane muffled the sound, but the guy out of sight said, "I don't give a damn," and the sergeant walked away while taking a sip from his bottle.

Dressed again like a teenage boy and not a pope, I exited the parish house through the basement door. I saw Tim talking to Jesse. "Yo!"

Tim turned in my direction. "Since Joni's in town, Katie wants me to bring you along tonight; maybe Joni will notice you this time."

"As long as you don't bring Audie Murphy with you, I might have a chance," I said, pointing at Jesse.

"Shit, man! I don't need no cross-carrying altar boy telling me what to do, and I can't come tonight anyway. The JAG major called a meeting at the armory," Jesse said in his interpretation of what a menacing black man would sound like. He wasn't very good at it.

"Can you get a car tonight? I can't," Tim asked.

"Yeah, I'll pick you up at seven thirty."

Chapter Nine
Key Club

The sky was a skullcap of darkness as I slowly pulled my car on to Katie's crescent driveway. Her house was big—really big. It had its own fire escape. It dominated one of the largest lots on one of Cumberland's most prestigious streets, the same street as Emmanuel Church, the county courthouse, and public library. If you lived on that street, you were somebody worth knowing. Of the late Victorian style, the house lurched upwards above miles of porch garishly adorned with wood filigree to a second floor of multiple gables jutting out at all angles. Above that was a tower topped with a mansard roof sheathed in gray slate. Morticia and Gomez Addams would have felt right at home here.

The Bandershots were big money in Cumberland. The colonel's family inherited hundreds of acres just in time to sell it to burgeoning industries crowding into Allegany county in the late nineteenth century. Water and railroads were must-haves back then, and the Bandershot land had access to both.

"Which one's Katie's room?" I asked Tim as I parked on the side of the driveway and killed the engine. There were at least ten other cars in front of me, and the house was glowing with activity on both levels.

"It's in the back on the second floor. Come on, I'll show you."

I followed Tim through the tree-lined south lawn which looked more like Central Park than private property.

"Jesus, who cuts all this grass?" I asked.

"Well, the colonel sure as shit didn't do it, nor anyone else with his last name. That kind of work is reserved for the hired help. There's Katie's room, on the corner of the second floor."

I could tell Tim knew his way around the place; he must have made this trip before. Katie's room was conveniently serviced by the metal fire escape only a few yards away from her window across a porch roof.

Tim went first. He darted from our cover to the corner of the house then slid along the back wall behind overgrown boxwoods till he reached the foot of the fire escape. By the time I joined him, Tim was already up the ladder and quietly crossing the roof of the back porch. As I began my climb, I saw men and women through the windows, with drinks in hand, chatting like at any cocktail party. You'd never know they were attending a wake. Just as I stepped onto the roof, the porch's door creaked open, and voices spilled out below me.

"You can't do that, Pat. You can't. It will kill me," said a man sounding like he was losing an argument. "Please wait and decide after things quiet down. It shouldn't be more than a month or two before this is all behind us."

I froze and looked at Tim to make sure he knew not to move. He did and was crouched against the wall of the house.

"We'll see," said a woman I had heard earlier that day give Katie an order. "There are too many people in this town who know too much about me, and I can't stand it."

Chapter Nine - Key Club

"I know, but I love you, Pat. Haven't I proven that by divorcing Jill? Now that Mike is dead, we're free to be together," the man pleaded.

"Are we?" Mrs. Bandershot asked sternly. "Fourteen people know about that club, and half of them are in my living room right now. I can feel their eyes on me."

The man's voice continued, "Remember, if it weren't for the key club, we wouldn't have found each other, and—"

"Don't ever mention that again!" Katie's mother cut him off like a guillotine. "Don't ever say it again. That little man made me join that club, and I hated him for it, and worst of all, now that he's gone, there's no reason for others to keep the secret."

"Well, at least you have his money and the prestige of his military service," the man said, trying to calm the situation.

"Ha!" Pat Bandershot laughed so loud I felt it through my feet.

"There's no money. That idiot lost it all when he bought land near Rocky Gap and built that goddamn marina. He was sure the water-tourist industry was the future of Cumberland and the lake they were putting out there would be the big draw. He envisioned hundreds of houses filled with summer tourists, all water skiing and all needing a place to buy and store boats. Then the state stepped in and declared the lake a reservoir that wouldn't allow either housing or motor boats. No houses, no tourists. No boats, no need for a marina."

"Pat, I'm so sorry, I didn't know that. It was all before I moved to town," the calmer voice said. "How much did he lose?"

"Over two million, and he borrowed a lot of it. When the half-built marina failed, the bank forced us into bankruptcy. We lost the building and the land. Christ, they even own half of this goddamn house."

"What about his military retirement? As a colonel in the Maryland National Guard, he must have drawn a decent salary, didn't he?"

"The National Guard is a hospice where military reputations go to die, and Mike's was on life support before he joined. Oh, he got paid for it, and I'll get his pension, but it isn't much."

The sound of glass shattering filled the air.

"Shit! I've dropped my goddamn drink. Get me another one. I can't face the rest of this night without it," the grieving widow ordered.

"Pat, the military owes you. The colonel was a hero of D-Day, wasn't he?"

"Just another lie," said Katie's mother. "He was on Omaha Beach all right, but he got knocked silly five minutes into it and was found twelve hours later, half naked in a hedgerow. The Army relieved him of command and shipped him home. He later transferred to the National Guard in hope of hanging on long enough to retire. The man was nothing but ten miles of bad road. The only good thing he's done recently is getting himself shredded by a grenade. A murder means I'll collect double on his life insurance."

"Oh, Pat, that's horrible," the man said.

Chapter Nine - Key Club

"If you don't get me that drink, I'll do it myself," Pat Bandershot said with the warmth of an iceberg.

I heard the porch door open, slam shut, and then reopen and close again. I waited a few seconds then moved over near Tim.

"Did you hear all that?" I whispered.

"Yeah, but what's a key club?"

"I don't know. Maybe it's like the Playboy Club where members get a key."

"Maybe, but there's no Playboy Club in Cumberland. We're lucky we have an Elks Club," Tim said, trying not to laugh. "Hey, one thing. We can't mention this to Katie. She may not know about the bankruptcy or her mother and that guy, and I don't think we should tell her, at least not yet."

"Right," I said.

Tim spun on the balls of his feet and moved closer to Katie's bedroom window. The pop sounds of the song "I Think I Love You" pulsed through the glass.

"Tim, you need to rethink this. Katie listens to *The Partridge Family*," I said.

"I don't care if she likes opera as long as she's my girl." Tim tapped twice on the pane with his class ring.

Joni's face appeared, and she opened the window.

I clutched my hands over my heart. "But soft, what light through yonder window breaks?"

"Tis the fair maid Joni, good sir; Juliet's down the hall in the bathroom."

"You'll do," I said as we squeezed through the curtained opening one at a time.

The high-ceilinged room was huge with beautiful carved furniture. Katie's bed was big, but it was dwarfed by an oversized wardrobe, chest of drawers, and matching vanity. She even had a Victorian rocking chair and love seat tucked in one corner.

I ran my hand along the top of the vanity. "This place looks like a museum."

"If it is, then the colonel and Aunt Pat are the statues," Joni said.

"What do you mean?" Tim asked.

"This is not a *Brady Bunch* happy family. I don't know how Katie stands it. Although Aunt Pat's a bitch, she does care for Katie, but the colonel wanted a boy and never looked at her as anything more than a liability. Katie gave up on him years ago."

The bedroom door opened, and in walked Katie with a six-pack of beer tucked under her peasant's blouse.

"I figured we could use a little refreshment," she said as she lifted her top to remove the cans. "Mom won't miss this. It's from Dad's den refrigerator."

"She's a keeper," I said to Tim.

Tim put his arm around Katie and squeezed her tight. "I know. C'mon, babe. Let's get out of here."

Chapter Ten
A Suspect

Katie didn't waste any time. She had a beer opened and was drinking it before we got to the car.

"If I never come back to this house, it will be too soon," she said as she dropped into the back seat of my Barracuda with Tim squeezing in after her.

Trying to change the subject, I asked, "Hey, girls, do you want to have a campfire at the cave?"

"Sure," both girls answered.

There were a few lights on in the armory as we passed it, but the gym was dark. Tim escorted the girls through the woods as I gathered firewood.

We had a fire going and were enjoying our beer when we heard branches rustling outside. Someone was entering the cave. A dark shadow rose up from the entrance, and Katie gasped.

"I thought it was you guys," Jesse said as he brushed leaves from his coat. "I went for a walk to clear my head after that crazy meeting tonight and smelled your campfire."

"Hi, big guy," Joni said as she stood and hugged Jesse. The top of her head barely reached his chin. Katie did the same as I looked at Tim and rolled my eyes.

"Want a beer?" Tim asked.

"No, I've got to get home and help Dad. If I smell like beer, he won't let me."

"So, what was crazy about your meeting?" I asked.

"I don't know why I was there. All I did was fix coffee, so I didn't get to hear everything, but I think the major is planning on charging someone with the murder."

Katie pulled on Jesse's coat. "Who?"

"I don't know, but they're gonna do it soon. The major kept going around and around asking questions about a suspect's motive, means, and opportunity, but I didn't hear any names. The police chief was there tonight, and the major has asked him to help with the arrest. He said he needed some paperwork first, something from our files. The major ordered Sergeant Inversol to find it. He spent the entire meeting in another office searching for it. In fact, he's still in there now."

"Jack's in the armory?" Katie asked.

"Yeah, everyone else has gone home," Jesse said.

Katie tossed her second empty beer can down. "I want to see Jack. I've been visiting him in that place since I was three years old. He was my babysitter when Dad was supposed to be watching me. I love him like an uncle."

"Okay, I can let you in the front door, but I've got to get home," Jesse said.

Tim stood. "Hey, won't he tell your mom you snuck out?"

Chapter Ten - A Suspect

"No, he's on my side," Katie said as she grabbed Tim's hand and pulled him towards the cave's opening. Jesse and Joni followed them.

I picked up a stick. "I'll catch up with you in a minute. I need to put out the fire."

I was stirring the fire and watching its last light flicker off the walls when I noticed something odd near the back of the cave. I squinted into the dark and saw neatly stacked lumber.

"That wasn't here last time," I said out loud and wondered why anyone would store lumber in a cave.

I was about to turn on my flashlight and take a closer look when Joni called, "Shelby, what are you doing in there? I'm getting cold."

"Coming!" I yelled and headed for the opening, excited that Joni was waiting for me.

Jesse was unlocking the front door of the armory as Joni and I arrived. Tim was the first to go in.

As he crossed the threshold, the lights in the armory's entry hall flipped on, and Tim backed up with his hands over his head. "Don't shoot."

Sergeant Inversol leaned on a wall with his left hand on a light switch and his right hand pointing a .45-caliber pistol at us.

"Stay right where you are, boy, this is Uncle Sam's house, and I'm guarding it for him."

"Jack, don't shoot. It's Katie."

"Kit-Kat is that you, sweetie?" Inversol said as he lowered his gun. "What in the name of Jehovah are you doing here, girl?"

Sergeant Jack Inversol was nearing fifty and not an easy man to look at. His height was average, but his weight was not. He was more seed bag than sinew. His gray hair was thin and his nose splotchy as if it had once caught fire and was put out with an ice pick.

Katie ran across the hall and hugged the bear of a man. "I came to see you, Jack. With Daddy gone, you're all I've got."

"Now, Kit-Kat, that ain't true. You've got your mom to take care of you."

"She doesn't understand me, Jack. I can't talk to her. She only wants to tell me what to do."

"Okay, I understand, but what are you doing up here, girl? We just put your daddy in the ground this morning."

"My friends are helping me get my mind off that," Katie said.

"What friends are those?" Jack asked, looking up from Katie's face for the first time.

"Well, you already know Jesse," Katie said.

Sergeant Inversol's eyes burned on Jesse. "Corporal Preslor, you being a good soldier around my Kit-Kat?"

"Yes, Sergeant."

"And this is Joni, my cousin," Katie continued, pulling Joni forward by the hand.

Chapter Ten - A Suspect

"Well, how do you do, missy?" A smile crackled across Jack's face.

"And the boys are Tim and Shelby, my friends from the band."

The sergeant shook first Tim's then my hand, and I got a definite whiff of bourbon when he did.

Jack leaned against the light switch wall again as if he needed the support. "What can I do for you?"

"Nothing, Jack. I just wanted to see you. Why are you working so late tonight? I know you've had a long day."

Sergeant Inversol's head dropped, and he got an unpleasant look on his face like he didn't want to answer.

"I'm helping find out who killed your daddy, Kit-Kat. There's a lot to be done and—"

Jack was interrupted by the sound of car doors closing. We turned towards the front door as they burst open, and in flooded five police officers. They were all armed, and those arms were pointed at us as they boxed us in.

No one said a word until two more uniformed men came in and pushed through the line of police. I recognized the Army rank of major on the shoulder epaulets of the one man, but the other guy had stars pinned to the lapels of his dark Cumberland policeman's uniform.

"I'm Major Bennington, and this is Chief Thompkins. As a duly appointed member of the Judge Advocate Corps, I have an arrest warrant for Sergeant John Thomas Inversol."

Slippery When Wet

Major Bennington could have been the prototype for Hasbro's G.I. Joe doll: perfect and plastic. On the other hand, Chief Thompkins was squat and square: more Fred Flintstone than action figure.

Jack didn't move from his wall, and as the major saw the sergeant's sidearm, he pointed his pistol at him and said, "I'll take that, Inversol. Let's not make this any harder than it already is."

"Preslor, did you know about this?" Jack said to Jesse, ignoring the major.

The major answered, "No, Sergeant, nobody knew about this except for me, but you've been my prime suspect from the very beginning, and you know why. You have the right to remain silent. Should you give up that right, anything you say may be used against you in a court of law. You also have the right to an attorney. Do you understand this?"

Time stopped as we waited for the sergeant's answer.

"Yes, sir," Sergeant Inversol said sadly, as his right hand lifted his gun out towards the major, grip first, and his left hand flipped off the light switch.

Katie screamed, and Major Bennington yelled, "No!" as blackness engulfed us all. I heard scuffling and dropped to the floor, thinking down was the safest direction. A gunshot exploded. Its concussive wave pulsed through me followed by echoed ringing in my ears. My hearing felt thick as if the room was full of water. Someone tripped over me as everyone scrambled to survive a few seconds more.

Chapter Ten - A Suspect

Somebody yelled, "I've got him," and a fist smacked flesh. The lights came back on.

Two cops were wrestling each other, and Bennington was standing alone in the center of the room holding Jack's gun. In his other hand was his still smoking pistol. There was blood on the floor, but the sergeant was gone.

"Freeze, everyone, freeze!" the major ordered, holstering his weapon. "He's not going anywhere. I've got police on all the exits."

The chief yelled into a walkie-talkie, "All units, report, suspect escaped, may be armed and dangerous."

The walkie-talkie crackled with static. One by one, the police stationed at the exits checked in.

They had heard the gunshot but saw nothing, and no one left through their doors. The chief looked at Major Bennington and said, "He's got to be in the building."

Tim had joined me on the floor, and our eyes locked as we began to breathe again. Jesse had pulled Katie and Joni against a wall and was shielding them with his body.

"Get every goddamn light on in this place and search it from top to bottom. Preslor, take the civilians into that office and keep them there!" yelled the major.

Policemen scattered, and Jesse pushed us into Colonel Bandershot's office.

The room had a low ceiling and was filled with uncomfortable but efficient furniture. A large desk sat to our left flanked by

American and Maryland flags. Behind it was a wall of books with a collection of cameras displayed between volumes. Katie, Joni, and Tim sat down on a couch below the window as Jesse sat at one of the six metal chairs surrounding an oval table.

Jesse tilted back in his chair. "We might as well make ourselves comfortable. This could take a while."

"What just happened out there?" Joni asked with a stunned voice.

"I don't know. Let's just do what the major says and wait quietly in here," Tim answered.

My hands felt dirty from the armory's floor. I didn't see any blood on me, but the possibility of it made me queasy. I opened a door on the far wall that I thought was a bathroom, hoping to wash my hands, and found myself in a closet-like room, only there were no hangers or clothes.

"What's this?" I asked as I flipped on the lights. Instead of the standard white light, everything was bathed in a reddish-yellow glow.

The room was lined on both sides with waist-high workbenches. It smelled like my chemistry teacher's lab at school. On the left bench were three good-sized pans aligned neatly from left to right with what looked like a clothesline with clips strung above it. Neatly labeled gallon-size bottles lined the other bench along with stacks of very thick paper. At the far end of the room on the largest of the work areas was a small sink and what looked like an overhead projector,

Chapter Ten - A Suspect

only different. It had a bulbous top with lenses affixed below it that pointed down onto a flat plate.

Jesse joined me. "That's the colonel's darkroom. He fancied himself an amateur photographer. It was installed up here a while ago after he damn near burned his house down mixing the wrong chemicals. Don't touch anything, or I'll catch hell."

Jesse let me wash my hands, then pulled me out, and closed the door, and I joined him at the conference table to wait.

"Hey, there are some pretty neat cameras here," Tim said, having walked over to the wall of books. "Wow, look at this one! It's just like the spy camera James Bond used in *On Her Majesty's Secret Service*." Tim held up what looked like a silver pack of gum.

"Put that down," Jesse said, sounding like Tim's mother. "We're already in some deep shit, let's not wade into more."

After about an hour, the police found nothing and expanded their search beyond the armory. There was no sign of Sergeant Inversol. The only indication he had been there at all was a trail of blood that led down the hallway to the men's room, but it ended there. Jack had disappeared.

The major was not happy. We heard him tell the police chief to issue an APB and notify all train and bus stations and to search Inversol's YMCA room.

Major Bennington came into the colonel's office. "I need you all to go home now, but I'll want to talk to you later. Jesse, lock up the armory for me. I'll have a team clean it up later. I don't know where that son-of-a-bitch sergeant is, but I'll find him."

"Yes, Major."

A frown smeared the major's face as he looked up at the ceiling, huffed, and walked out the door.

Jesse disappeared down the hall to turn off the lights, and we moved into the front room to wait for him. Sergeant Inversol's blood was still there, but it looked as if someone had used it as finger paint to decorate the floor. We went outside.

Jesse found us there and said, "Well, that was something."

"I can't believe the major shot Jack," Katie said as she held back tears. "And why were they arresting him? He wouldn't kill Dad. Dad was the only reason he had a job here. No one else would hire him with his problem."

"Are you talking about this?" Jesse asked as he removed a good-sized medicine bottle from the pocket of his fatigue jacket and handed it to Katie.

Katie looked at it and read aloud from the label. "Morphine sulfate oral solution, fifteen milligrams per five milliliters." She nodded. "Yes, Jack needs that for his pain. He doesn't think I know about it, but I've seen him pour it into his bourbon. I think he got a doctor to prescribe a little bit for him, but he has someone getting more for him on the side. I've heard him on the phone talking about it. He calls it his nerve medicine."

"What's wrong with him?" I asked.

Chapter Ten - A Suspect

"Jack was hit by fragments from an artillery shell during the Battle of the Bulge. He spent two years in and out of veterans' hospitals after that, but they never were able to get all of the metal out of his back. I don't think he is ever really without pain."

Jesse took the bottle back. "Well, this is just one of two bottles he's got stashed in his office. I looked around in there a bit and found them under a stack of papers in a desk drawer. I was going to take it to a pharmacist friend and see if Jack had a prescription, but I guess I don't have to do that now."

Tim took the bottle and looked at it and then up at me. "This stuff will kill you if you're not careful. It takes away your pain but also suppresses the respiratory system. One teaspoon too much and you go to sleep and never wake up. My dad told me about it when he prescribed it for our neighbor with terminal cancer. It's not something you take to get better."

"Your dad's a doctor?" Joni asked.

"Tim's father is the most respected surgeon in Cumberland," I said, knowing Tim would never boast about his dad.

"What do we do now?" Katie asked.

"We go home."

Chapter Eleven
I Didn't Do It

Sleep came in spurts that night. Every time I'd drift off, the shooting would replay in my head, ending with the image of the bloodstained floor. I kept asking myself, "What are you getting yourself into?" And I didn't like the answer.

My phone rang, and I saw that it was after nine o'clock in the morning. "Hello," I said unsteadily.

"Come down to my house. Katie's here, and she's heard from Inversol," Tim said.

"I'll be right there."

Tim only lived four doors down the road from me, and when I arrived at his side door, I saw a brand-new Cadillac Eldorado parked unevenly in front of his house.

I walked in and found him sitting on the couch in his dad's den with Katie.

"Where's Joni?" I asked.

"She and my aunt and uncle left this morning just before I got the call," Katie said.

"From Sergeant Inversol?"

"Yes, he wanted me to know he was all right."

"Did he get shot?" I asked.

Chapter Eleven - I Didn't Do It

"Yes, the bullet nicked his right thigh, but he stopped the bleeding and had his morphine supplier stitch him up. He also got a fresh supply of his nerve medicine," Katie said.

"Where is he?"

"He wouldn't tell me, but he wanted me to know he didn't kill Dad. He was adamant. He kept saying 'I didn't do it, I didn't do it. I've done some bad things, but I could never kill my commanding officer.'"

I moved nearer to Katie. "What's he going to do?"

"I don't know, but he talked about cleaning up some loose ends. Should I tell the police?"

Tim had his arm around Katie's shoulder and was rocking her a bit as she sobbed. "Let's wait a while before we decide. You are already mixed up in this thing enough."

Katie looked up and wiped her eyes. "Okay, I've got to get home before Mom realizes I took her car. She was blotto again last night and on the phone ranting to someone about her reputation."

I glanced at Tim, and his tight-lipped look willed me into silence.

Monday came and went, and I endured school. The newspapers were alive with headlines telling everything they knew about the shooting and the attempted arrest of Sergeant Inversol. I absorbed it all and stole my dad's copy of the Tuesday morning paper so I could read it first. With no new news to report, the paper had short biographies on everyone involved in the case, including Police Chief Russ Thompkins, Major Stan Bennington, and suspect number one: Sergeant Jack Inversol.

A native of Cumberland, Jack dropped out of high school his junior year to enlist in the Army. That's how he found himself on Omaha Beach in Colonel Bandershot's tank brigade. The article detailed Jack's life in full, the good and the bad. After the war, he was unable to hold a steady job due to his alcohol issues. He lived with his parents until they died then moved to the YMCA. It wasn't until Colonel Bandershot became commander of the armory in 1959 that Jack got a steady job. He filled one of only two full-time positions there as the commander's administrative clerk.

Unlike Jack's bio, Major Bennington's read like a script for a movie about an all-American boy who made good. He was the top undergraduate at Boston College, then went to Yale Law, and then spent two tours in Vietnam on General Westmorland's JAG staff. He was a man on the move, and the direction was up.

Chief Thompkins's career wasn't as spectacular, but he had succeeded enough to become the youngest chief of police Cumberland ever had. He got the job at thirty-nine with the help of some locally powerful men who recognized his potential.

I was rereading the paper at the side of the band room while waiting for practice to start. Dad called for everyone to quiet down then made some announcements.

Chapter Eleven - I Didn't Do It

Tim was sitting with his baritone ready to play, and I saw Katie and the other twirlers to the right of the band, waiting for the rehearsal to move outside for marching practice.

"Excuse me, Lu, I'm sorry to interrupt, but I need to see your son, Tim Lewis, and Katie Bandershot out in the hall immediately," said Vice Principal Ron Chapman. He had come in and walked right up beside Dad without anyone noticing. Vice principals are good at that.

I heard a metal crash and saw Tim reaching down to retrieve the baritone horn that had slipped out of his hands. I stood and moved towards him.

"Right, Ron," Dad said. "Katie, Shelby, Tim, you go with the vice principal." Having heard her name, Katie started to move but looked unsteady. Tim grabbed her arm and led her out the door. Waiting for us in the hall was Chief of Police Thompkins.

"Let's go over here away from the band room door so we have some privacy. I need to tell you something before the reporters get to you. But first, I want to ask you a few questions. Have any of you heard from Sergeant Inversol since the shooting?"

I felt my back stiffen as if a concrete truck was pouring a load down my spine. Tim looked as if he'd been stricken with lockjaw.

"Yes, I have," said Katie.

"When?" the chief asked.

"Sunday morning."

"What did he tell you?"

"That he was all right and he didn't kill Dad. He didn't tell me where he was or what he was going to do next. Honest," Katie said without emotion.

"Have either of you two boys heard from him?" the chief asked.

"No, sir," Tim and I answered together. "But we knew Katie talked with him," Tim added.

I winced in pain as Chief Thompkins got that look on his face my mother got whenever I disappointed her.

I felt Dad's hands on my shoulders. He had come into the hall to see what this was all about.

Chief Thompkins paused, took a deep breath, and then said, "Okay, I've got some bad news. Early this morning, Sergeant Inversol was found dead in his office at the armory of an apparent suicidal overdose. Your friend Jesse found him when he opened up the armory for the cleaning staff."

Katie slumped to the floor. Luckily, she was standing between Tim and me, so we cushioned her fall.

We all bent down at once, bumping into each other. Dad removed his jacket and put it under her head.

"What's this all about?" he whispered in my ear.

"I'll tell you everything later."

Chapter Eleven - I Didn't Do It

"The armory. Inversol was found in the armory?" I asked the chief.

He removed his hat and scratched his squarish head. "Yes, we thought he'd escaped, but he must have been hiding in there all this time."

"Are you sure it's a suicide?" Tim asked. "The sergeant told Katie he didn't kill the colonel, and if he didn't do it, why would he kill himself?"

"It looks that way, and the note he left makes things pretty clear. I can't tell you anything else; I just didn't want you to be jumped by reporters who will be looking for all the angles on what is turning out to be the biggest story of the year. Lu, I suggest you get these kids home as soon as you can," counseled Chief Thompkins.

"Right. Ron, can you handle band for me?" Dad said to the silent vice principal who had secretly joined us.

"Sure, Lu, as long as I don't have to march."

Chapter Twelve
The Case is Closed

Our lives went into semi-hibernation with the news of Sergeant Inversol's death. Katie's mother whisked her off to Massachusetts for two weeks of hiding with relatives, Tim and I laid low, and Jesse became invisible.

Inversol was only cold for twenty-four hours before Major Bennington held a press conference announcing the Colonel Bandershot murder case was solved. He had indisputable evidence pointing to Inversol's guilt. He provided photostats of the suicide note along with documents detailing the sergeant's access to the grenades and the tank prior to the crime. Sworn testimonies were also obtained from other guardsmen of his long-standing dislike of the colonel.

The major stated with great certainty, "The sergeant had a clear motive, means, and opportunity to commit the crime and has admitted guilt in his suicide note."

The next day's newspaper headlines screamed Major Bennington's conclusion: "The case is closed," along with pictures of Inversol slumped over his desk and his suicide note. It read: "Forgive me for betraying the only thing in this world that cared for me—the U.S. Army. I plan to make amends."

Soon afterward, Jack Inversol was buried without honors at the local veterans' cemetery with only the gravedigger and funeral home staff in attendance.

Chapter Twelve - The Case is Closed

Major Bennington returned to Washington, Inversol's office was locked until someone could arrange to clean it out, and National Guard headquarters assigned an acting commander.

The shock wore off, and normality returned.

It was the first Saturday of the last month of the year, and I was only minutes away from finishing a six-hour afternoon shift at the Tastee Freez when the manager told me there was someone at the back door wanting to talk to me. I put down the scraping tool I was using to clean the hamburger grill, wiped my hands on my apron, and walked to the back door.

The sun was gone, and so was my visitor, but as I began to close the door, I heard, "Syckes, over here."

I glanced right to where the big green dumpster sat radiating odors only fast food trash could produce and saw Jesse motioning me to come that way.

"What the hell, Jesse? Come on in the store."

"No, I need to talk to you in private. When do you get off?"

"I'm getting off now. Let me sign out and get my coat; it's freezing out here."

"Okay, I'm parked across the street behind the gas station. I'll wait for you there," Jesse said and backed into the darkness.

As I approached Jesse's VW, I saw him in the back seat illuminated by a glowing cigarette. I tapped on the hatch-like side door, and Jesse fumbled with the handle for a few seconds before opening it.

Slippery When Wet

"The latch is weak, so I back it up with a bungee cord," Jesse said as a cloud of suspicious-smelling smoke billowed out from the door. I stepped up into the microbus and sat in the jump seat across from Jesse.

"I see you are enjoying some of your product tonight," I said, coughing at the coarse, burned marijuana cloud.

"Business is way off with all the shit going down at the armory, and I need a little weed to take the edge off. You want some? It's some super special dope. I got it off a brother just back from the Philippines, and it's got some magic mushroom ground up in it to free your consciousness."

"No thanks. I want to keep my consciousness locked up right now. What's with all the sneaking around?"

Jesse took a long toke on his diminishing reefer. "You see, when a black man has shit on white men, he needs to be careful—especially if two of the white men are dead."

I shook my head. "What are you talking about?"

"Look at this," he said, handing me a manila envelope. I grabbed the wrong end of the envelope, and the contents spilled onto the floor of the bus, scattering into a collage, an explosive collage.

"Jesus!" I gasped. There spread out at my feet were half-a-dozen eight-by-ten glossy black-and-white photographs of naked men and women engaged in creative sex acts. I bent down and gathered the lurid photos and flipped through them one by one.

Chapter Twelve - The Case is Closed

My mind was spinning trying to comprehend what I was seeing. The photos were not professional shots: the lighting was harsh, and the photographer was apparently on the move as the pictures were taken. Subjects appeared at odd angles and not always in focus, but in most cases, it was clear who they were.

I recognized several of the men. There was a prominent doctor, a bank manager, and I think the guy with the cowboy hat on was a county judge. Each photo had a different male subject, but the woman in every picture was the same. Only one lady has thirty-eight D-cups like that: Pat Bandershot.

The photos weren't taken at the same place or time. Mrs. Bandershot's negligee was different from photo to photo—when she had one on at all. I let them drop into my lap and looked into Jesse's face. "Where did you get these?"

"You know I was the one who found Inversol's body. Well, that envelope was on his desk right next to his suicide note, and when I saw what was inside, I decided to take it. I don't know why, but I did."

"But, Jesse, how did Inversol get these? Was he spying on Mrs. Bandershot?"

"No, I think the colonel took the photos; he's the big photography nut. Inversol must have stolen them from him. Who knows, maybe he was blackmailing the colonel."

There was a long silence between us as we both realized the implications of that possibility.

"Why would Inversol kill his golden goose?" I asked. "I mean, if you're blackmailing a guy for money, the last thing you want to do is blow him up in a tank."

"You're right. That doesn't make a damn bit of sense," Jesse added. "And if you didn't kill a guy, you sure as shit wouldn't kill yourself because he's dead."

I was shaking my head and looking down at the photos. "It doesn't add up. If Inversol killed Bandershot and then killed himself because of the guilt from the terrible thing he did, why would he leave photos lying around that would further hurt that man's family?"

Jesse continued my thought. "And why would you sign a suicide note saying you're sorry and you plan to make amends? Leaving behind photos of your victim's wife getting banged by half the country club is not making amends."

Jesse's comment on the note exploded in my head. "Wait, did you say Inversol's suicide note was signed? The photostat printed in the paper didn't show a signature."

"I know," said Jesse, "But it was signed. Look, I made a copy of it on the armory's machine before I called the police."

He handed me the copy of the suicide note, and it contained the same two lines as the one in the newspaper. It also had Sergeant Inversol's weak cursive signature in thick ink, but that wasn't all. Just to the right of the signature was a blotchy stain followed by a straight line and finally two poorly drawn symbols: a triangle and a zero with a line through it from top to bottom like the Europeans do.

Chapter Twelve - The Case is Closed

"What do those mean?" I asked.

"Shit if I know. Is that an A and an O or some doodling, and what's with that big stain?" Jesse asked.

"You don't doodle when you're dying."

I handed the photos and the note back to Jesse, but he waved me off. "No way, man! I came here to give them to you, and I've done that. If a brother is found with that kind of kinky-white-man shit on him, he's lynched before sundown."

"But what am I going to do with them?" I asked.

"Dress them up like rodeo clowns, I don't care. Listen, I know we need to do something with these, but I can't be the one who does it. I'm not abandoning you, but I can't be the lead singer on this song."

I didn't answer, but I knew Jesse was right. Cumberland may have integrated its schools, but lots of people still didn't trust the "coloreds."

Jesse lifted his head like he was trying to see over a wall. "I feel like I'm in an overflowing toilet. We better find a plunger, or we're going to drown."

"I hear that, but why are two people dead, and more importantly, why is the case associated with those deaths closed?"

Chapter Thirteen
A Closer Look

When I got home, I called Tim. "Hey, have you still got that lighted magnifying stand, the one with four legs that you can place things under?"

"Yeah, my dad uses it with his stamp collection."

"Bring it up to my house, will you? I've got something we need to look at up close and without any of your little brothers around."

It was after seven before Tim showed up with the magnifier, and with my parents out for the evening, we had the house to ourselves.

"Come on down to the basement. You're not going to believe what I've got spread out on the pool table," I said to Tim, handing him a beer I'd borrowed from my dad's stock.

I heard him pop the top of the can as we went down the stairs, and I moved to the far side of the pool table so I could see his expression when he saw the pictures I'd carefully laid out.

"Wowzer! Those are some seriously big tits," Tim gushed as he sucked on the top of his beer. "Holy cow, is that who I think it is?"

"Yes, it is."

"Does Katie know about these?" Tim asked.

Chapter Thirteen - A Closer Look

"No, and I'm bound and determined to keep it that way."

Tim picked up one of the most salacious of the photos. "I agree. Wait, that's my mom's gynecologist with his…in her…Well, let's just say it isn't where it's supposed to be," Tim continued as he leaned over the pool table and unfolded the legs of the magnifying stand.

"I know, but you're looking at all the obvious stuff. I think there is a lot more in these photos I want to check out with that gadget of yours," I said, taking it from him. "I've written down what I've found so far, but I think there's more if we can bring into focus some of the stuff in the background."

I filled Tim in on how I'd gotten the photos and everything Jesse and I discussed, but Tim's mind was focused on something else.

"Shelby, do you think this is the key club Mrs. Bandershot was talking about the other night?"

"Crap, I'd forgotten about that. I don't know. Maybe? She was pretty sure her reputation was on the line if information about that club got out. If this is it, she's got reason to worry."

"This is just really crazy. I mean, this is Cumberland for God's sake! We're so buttoned-up you can't even buy gas on Sundays," Tim replied.

We started taking turns scouring each photo from side to side and top to bottom and listing whatever we found on a notepad.

Slippery When Wet

I had already written down everyone's name I recognized, and Tim added more to the list. He also noticed that one room in the photos looked like a cabin at a lake because waterskis were hanging on the wall. I confirmed what we already assumed—that Colonel Bandershot was the photographer when I saw his mustached face reflected in a mirror behind an action scene. He was holding that little spy camera up to his eye and had a massive smile on his face. But, the most sobering data point we stumbled upon was when I zoomed in on a dark shirt hanging from a chair in the only picture that did not show the face of the male participant. There on the shirt's right lapel were general officer stars. Chief of Police Thompkins was a key club member.

The realization that our city's legal authority in charge of the murder case was a member of a sex club with the murdered man's wife chilled us. Tim dropped the photo he was holding, and as he bent down to pick it up, he noticed a name and a phone number penciled on the back of it.

He read it aloud, "Ed—722-5257."

"What did you say?" I asked.

"There's a name and phone number on this photo, Ed—722-5257."

I was already dialing the number on the basement phone as Tim finished. The phone only rang twice before a gruff male voice answered, "Parkview Liquors."

I hung up without saying a word.

Chapter Fourteen
Backups

I pulled into the parking lot behind the public library and looked at Tim. "Okay, remember the plan. Get in and get out fast."

"Right," Tim said patting his three-ring binder. "I've got the photos in here."

We had decided the pictures were so powerful we couldn't risk losing them without a backup copy. Tim asked Jesse if we could use the armory's copy machine, but he refused to even discuss it. I also wanted to enlarge the scribbling at the bottom of the suicide note so I could show it to someone without revealing the source. The library had the only other copy machine available to us, and luckily, it enlarged as well as duplicated, but they charged a dime for every copy. That meant we had to involve the librarian; you had to pay her first. Tim's job was to make the copies. I was to make sure the librarian didn't see those photos.

The library loomed large as we passed through its Doric-columned entrance. I went to the card catalog, pulled open a drawer at random, and started flipping through cards. Tim went up to the unattended main desk, and seeing a domed call bell, he tapped the top twice. "Ding, ding," rang out, and a voice from the stairwell called, "Coming."

I saw Dorothy Dove step off the staircase with a load of books in her arms, and I knew we were in trouble. Dorothy did not tolerate fools easily, and she considered any teenage boy a fool. Tall and slender with a puckish round face, Dorothy loved her books and her library, and that's how she viewed the public establishment—as hers.

"Yes?" was all she said as she dropped her load of books on the counter and looked at Tim.

"I need to make copies of my biology notes so I can share them with a sick friend," Tim said.

"How many copies?" Dorothy asked as she reached down below the counter and retrieved a small notebook neatly titled Copy Log.

"Seven, but one of them is an enlargement," Tim answered.

"What on earth do you need to enlarge from your biology notes?" the ever-logical Dorothy asked.

Tim's face went blank. We hadn't anticipated needing to justify anything.

"Excuse me, where is the boys' room?" I asked, coming to Tim's rescue.

"All the way in the back of the building to the right. You'll need to turn the lights on first, though. The switch is on the wall," Dorothy said while leaving the counter and pointing down the hall.

"Thanks," I said and moved in the direction of her index finger, but I didn't go all the way. I hid in the shadows so I could help Tim if needed.

Chapter Fourteen - Backups

Tim spread two quarters and four nickels onto the counter. "So, that's seventy cents total for the seven copies?"

"Okay, get your material ready, and I'll turn the copier on for you in a second," Dorothy said as she slid the coins off into the palm of her hand, then opened the small notebook, and recorded the transaction.

The library's Xerox 4500 model was the latest in copying technology. Quiet and with two paper trays, it was the first copier in the world that could copy both sides of a document at once. The 4500 could even feed up to twenty pages into the machine for automatic copying. It was bigger than a golf cart.

Tim had a handful of biology notes out and was sorting them when Dorothy joined him at the machine. She used a key she kept around her neck to turn it on and then asked, "Do you want to use the automatic document feeder?"

"Is that the fastest way to make copies?" Tim asked.

"Yes."

Tim held up his notes. "Okay, but I don't want to use it for the enlargement of my drawing of a single-celled animal."

Dorthey leaned forward and turned a knob on the machine. "So that's what it is. You can do that first. You need to choose your enlargement percentage using this dial here then choose how many copies you want. I've already set it at one."

"Thanks, I've used the machine before. I think I can handle it," Tim assured her.

"Call me if you need any help," Dorothy said and turned back to the counter.

It was my turn to keep her busy while Tim did the copying.

"Mrs. Dove, Mom asked me to find a book for her, but I can't remember the exact title. It's the autobiography of a famous movie star from the 1940s. You know, the one who was married to another movie star?"

Dorothy looked at me with disdain. "What is this, *Jeopardy*? There were a lot of movie stars married to each other in the forties."

I pulled on my ear. "Sorry, I think she had a unique name like Lester or Pester or something like that and made a bunch of swimming movies."

"Esther Williams. You're talking about Esther Williams. She was married to Fernando Lamas; God he was gorgeous," Dorothy exclaimed while rolling her eyes upwards. "The book's called *The Million Dollar Mermaid,* and you'll find it in the upstairs stacks, fourth row down on the left side."

"Thanks," I said and turned to see how Tim was doing as Dorothy returned to her pile of books. He'd already successfully enlarged the right corner of the suicide note and was carefully sliding the six black-and-white photos into the automatic feed tray. Tim gave me a thumbs-up, and I climbed the stairs to find a book about a mermaid.

I heard the Xerox machine engage with a click then a swooshing sound, as it pulled each of the photos individually down the feed tray and onto the copy plate. I counted them

Chapter Fourteen - Backups

as they went: one, two, three, four, five, and then it stopped. The sound changed to a whirring then a buzzing before it fell silent. The final photo had jammed face-up in the feeding mechanism.

Tim made a yip-like noise, and I moved out to the balcony that looked down onto the main floor of the library to see what was happening. I saw Dorothy moving in Tim's direction as he frantically tried to retrieve the jammed photo of a nude Pat Bandershot down on all fours with a county judge riding her like a bucking bronco.

Dorothy was only steps away from Tim when I jumped up to the top shelf of the bookcase and pulled as many volumes off as I could. The shelf gave way, and no fewer than forty books crashed over me, pushing me back onto the floor. I screamed, and I was not pretending.

Dorothy looked up and ran for the stairs. She turned into my row and said, "What have you done?"

I was pushing books off my chest and legs. "Sorry, Mrs. Dove, I tried to reach the top shelf, and it gave way when I pulled on it. I'll help you put them away."

"No, you've done enough damage. It's going to take me an hour to restock the shelves, and I doubt you can help. Do you even know the Dewey Decimal System?"

"No, ma'am, I was never good with fractions. I'll get out of your way and look for Mom's book another time," I said as I quickly left her with the pile of pulp fiction.

Slippery When Wet

Back in the car, Tim was looking over his work. "Well, I got five of the six photos copied. Will that do?"

"It will have to. How did the enlargement come out?"

Tim passed me a piece of paper. "You tell me. I covered up everything but the symbols and set the magnification at two hundred percent."

They looked good. The two scribbles were now about an inch tall. "We'll keep these separate from the photos. I don't want to be dragging porn shots of your girlfriend's mother around with me."

Tim started laughing. "Right, but how are we going to find out what the symbols are? I would not recommend you go back into the library for at least six months."

"Bruce Baker," was all I said.

Chapter Fifteen
Seeing Things

Bruce Baker was my Latin teacher and a unique human being. He did not fit Cumberland's educational norms; therefore, the rest of the Allegany faculty watched him carefully. His hair was long but not hippie long. It flowed over his head from ear to ear, creeping down the sides of his face and bunching at the bottom in an unkempt goatee. But it wasn't Bruce's appearance that made me sure he could help us. He was brilliant and fluent in at least three languages. If he didn't know what those symbols were, no one would.

Monday after school, I made my way to Mr. Baker's classroom with the enlarged copy of the suicide note's symbols hidden in my Latin textbook. I knocked on the doorframe and said, "Excuse me, Mr. Baker. Do you have a minute to spare?"

He said nothing but raised his hand and signaled me to enter. Bruce was looking out the window. As he turned, I saw why he was silent; he was eating a huge pastrami sandwich. Continuing to chew until his mouth was clear, Bruce waited and then said, "God, I miss the New York delicatessens! Cumberland doesn't know good pastrami from a cow pie. What can I do for you, young Master Syckes?"

"Do you know what these are?" I said as I removed the sheet of paper from my book and handed it to him.

He studied the symbols for a few seconds then turned the paper upside down. Then he lifted his glasses from his nose and moved his eyes closer. There was a little mustard making its way down his goatee.

"What do you think they are?" he asked me.

"Well, I think that pointy one might be an Egyptian hieroglyphic? My friend thinks the other one is a zero drawn the way the Europeans do with a line through it."

Bruce glanced up from the paper with a surprised look on his face. "You know, good sir, that does look a bit like the bread cone hieroglyph for life, only it's a bit too uniform. I'm impressed you would know about such things."

I smiled and wondered if I should admit I didn't know anything about bread cones. I only said it was Egyptian because it looked like a pyramid. "What else could it be?" I asked.

Bruce studied the symbols a few seconds longer, then looked up, and laughed. "It's Greek to me."

I paused, wondering if this was a total waste of time, then said, "That's the point, Mr. Baker. It's Greek to me too, but what do they mean?"

"No, Shelby, that's the answer. These aren't hieroglyphs; they're the Greek letters Delta and Phi."

"Delta Phi?" I questioned.

"Yes, I don't know why I didn't see it immediately. The triangle is the Greek letter Delta and the zero with the line

Chapter Fifteen - Seeing Things

through it, is the letter Phi. Delta Phi is a college fraternity," Bruce said as he handed the paper back to me.

"Thanks, Mr. Baker. I knew you were the right one to ask. I need to go tell my friend the news."

Leaving Mr. Baker to his sandwich, I went looking for Jesse. When I reached his house, his father said he was working at the church. I found him kneeling near the altar polishing brass fixtures.

"I hope you don't do all this work just because you're a good Christian," I said, walking down the center aisle.

"Man, I don't believe in anything but cold hard cash, and I'm the only one who gets paid for being on their knees in here," Jesse said, looking up.

"I hear that. Hey, I found out what those symbols are at the bottom of Inversol's note."

"Quiet, man, Reverend Cooper is wandering around here somewhere, and I don't want him knowing about any of that," Jesse said, standing and coming closer to me. "What are they?"

"They're Greek fraternity house letters, and the frat is Delta Phi."

"Well, that's crazy," Jesse said. "Jack Inversol didn't finish high school let alone go to college, and how do you know there is such a fraternity?"

"My Latin teacher told me, but I haven't checked it out otherwise. Hey, do you think someone else put those Greek letters on the note? Who knows, maybe Inversol didn't sign it at all and that's why the cops didn't publish it."

Jesse held up his polishing rag. "I thought about that, but I'm sure they compared that signature with things Inversol signed at the armory. Hey, I've got to finish polishing this stuff. Can we talk about this later?"

"Sure, how about we get together with Tim, drink some beer, and throw the Frisbees?"

"It's too cold to throw disks, and I'm off beer for a while. I'm taking a break from all things mind-altering after the other night. I smoked three more joints of that magic mushroom shit after you left, and it seriously screwed me up. I mean, I had an out-of-body experience or hallucination or something. Whatever it was, it scared me more than those naked pictures of that old white woman."

"Are you serious?" I asked Jesse.

"I'm as serious as a heart attack, and I damn near had one."

Jesse came down from the altar and sat with me on the front pew of the church.

"You know that story my dad told you about how my great-great-grandmother escaped slavery and gave birth in the tunnels just below us? Well, the other night, that old lady came to visit me."

"You talked to your great-great-grandmother who's been dead for forty-five years?" I asked incredulously.

Chapter Fifteen - Seeing Things

"Well, I didn't talk to her. She did all the talking, but it was as real as I'm talking to you right now."

Jesse's face turned somber.

"As I said, after you left, I smoked some more dope—too damn much dope—but I was feeling mellow. I had my Hendrix eight-track on the stereo, and everything was fine until my eyes went batshit crazy. I mean, I lost control of the horizontal, the vertical, everything. Then things went completely black, I mean jet-black, except for a small white dot that appeared on the horizon. It was like I was in a tunnel, and the other end of the tunnel was miles away. There was movement, but I wasn't moving. Then, in what felt like a sonic wave flashing over me, everything slammed forward, and I was sitting in the front seat of my bus driving down a road at night. But I wasn't driving because I was in the back seat, too, watching me drive. It was bizarre."

Jesse paused, looked away, and took a deep breath. Turning back to me, he said, "Now, I don't want you to think I've lost my mind, but it felt real. It wasn't like dreaming; I was living it. I was driving my microbus down a narrow road, looking out the windows with Jimi Hendrix's "All Along the Watchtower" pouring in my ears. I didn't see houses or farms along the road. No, I saw water. Walls of water rushing past me, but it wasn't like I was in a river or anything because I wasn't wet. The water was like shimmering blue light speeding along beside me. So, I'm driving the bus, turning the steering wheel, but the steering wheel wasn't connected to anything. It was right where it's supposed to be, but it was just floating there, and no matter how I turned it, the bus just kept going straight down the road. I couldn't stop it."

"Then I saw Sally, and she was wearing a bright yellow dress with black ribbons. She wasn't moving, just standing by the side of the road as the water rushed past her and I came closer. Then everything stopped as if the bus and the water had reached the end of a bungee cord, and I was thrown forward. Rebounding, I found myself in the back seat again, and Sally was in the front seat driving. She slowly turned around to look at me and then called my name. 'Jesse. Jesse. You take care, boy. It's slippery—slippery when wet,' she said. Turning back, she jerked the steering wheel hard right and then left, and then the bungee cord snapped back. It felt as if everything went into superfast rewind. The bus, the water, and I were all thrown backward along the road and into the tunnel. Then everything went black again. When I opened my eyes, I was curled up in a fetal position on the shelf above the bus's engine. It was morning, and my battery was dead."

"Wow," I said shaking my head. "That was some serious wild weed."

I leaned forward to say something else when I heard, "Shelby, I thought you only came to church when you have acolyte duty," said Reverend Cooper, who had crept up behind us quieter than a vice principal. Finley Cooper was in his late thirties with a bald spot that was beginning to look like a yarmulke. The contrast between it and his all-white, stiff,

Chapter Fifteen - Seeing Things

Episcopal clerical collar made him look like a rabbi with a neck brace.

"Come on, Reverend Cooper. I come to church more than most kids."

"I'm just giving you a hard time. What are you doing here today?" Reverend Cooper asked.

"I'm visiting with Jesse. He and I were talking about a friend of ours who's pledging a fraternity. Hey, Mr. Cooper, you went to college. Were you in a fraternity?"

Reverend Cooper looked around as if he was worried someone might overhear him. "I'll tell you if you promise not to tell the deacons. Yes, I was a member of Alpha Gamma Omega while an undergraduate, but that's all you're getting out of me. What goes on at college stays at college."

"Have you ever heard of a fraternity called Delta Phi?" I asked.

Reverend Cooper's nose pinched as he looked up at the ceiling, "Yes, there was a Delta Phi house at my school. We beat them in lacrosse my senior year. Why?"

"That's the frat our friend is pledging, and we weren't sure if it was real or not."

"It's real, my boy, it's real," Mr. Cooper said as he patted me on the head like a good dog and left. I looked back at Jesse and nodded, having confirmed the existence of Delta Phi.

"Are you going to be okay?" I asked.

"Yeah, it's cool, but I don't want to see Grandma Sally ever again."

I looked around to make sure Reverend Cooper was gone. Then I said, "Listen, I know you don't want to touch these, but I made a backup copy of the photos."

I took a white envelope out of my back pocket and held it up. "I want to hide them somewhere, just in case,"

"In case what?" Jesse asked nervously. "Shit, do you think people are looking for them?"

"I don't know, but I'm going to hide them here in the church. Do you know any good places?"

"No way! I don't want to know where you put them. If people are looking for them, they aren't going to find them through me." Jesse got up and moved back to his polishing.

"Okay," I said. "Listen, I've got another question for you. Tim and I overheard Pat Bandershot talking to a guy about something called a key club, and we think it ties in with the photos."

"Key club? You mean like the Knights of Columbus or Rotary?" Jesse asked.

"No, a club where men and women do what they're doing in these photos," I said, holding up the envelope.

"Car keys," Jesse said. "I think that's what you're talking about. It's wife swapping, and that's what's going on in those pictures. We have the colonel's set, you know, the ones of his wife. I bet that every guy in the photos has a set of pictures

Chapter Fifteen - Seeing Things

of their wives doing the horizontal mambo with the other guys."

"What do car keys have to do with it?" I asked, not believing we were having this conversation in my church.

"One of the guys has a party, and it's just like every other party with lots of music and booze, but at some point, the men throw their car keys into a bowl. Then, one by one, the wives pick a set of keys out. The car keys determine who has sex with who," Jesse said.

"Wife swapping," I said a bit louder than I should have.

Jesse stood up. "Yeah, it's how middle-aged couples spice things up, I guess."

I stood, too. "Well, it's creative. I'll let you get back to your work, but let's meet up for dinner later and think our next step through."

I looked around for someplace to hide the copied photos, and it didn't take me long to find one. There it was, the perfect place to stash a few sheets of paper. I knew no one would ever find them there because I'd been coming to this church for the last seventeen years, and I'd never seen anyone go near it.

I walked up the three red-carpeted steps, turned right, and went up another couple of steps to a beautifully embellished brass lectern. I scanned the church to make sure no one else was there, and then I lifted the oversized copy of the *King James Bible* and slid the envelope underneath it.

Chapter Sixteen
Puzzle Pieces

Tim and I met Jesse at seven at the Coney Island Restaurant. As we walked in, Jesse waved to us from a back booth.

"We'll order first," I called and moved to the counter with Tim.

"Give me two with everything and a cherry Coke," Tim said to Mr. Giatras, who was wiping his hands on a stained towel.

"You want chips with that?" he asked.

"No, just the wieners."

Giatras moved to his right to begin the process of creating the culinary masterpiece his family had been selling to Cumberlanders since 1918. "That'll be a dollar thirty-five."

"I'll have the same, but with a lemon Coke," I said, and our Greek chef nodded and stacked another two buns on his forearm.

Before we could blink, he'd slid four hot dogs into the buns, slathered them with a mustard stick and topped them with sauce and ground onions. His work done, he smiled broadly under his fluffy mustache.

We paid and went to sit with Jesse.

Jesse slapped the table. "Two? Is that all you toddlers can handle—two little wieners? Four's my minimum and six my usual."

Chapter Sixteen - Puzzle Pieces

"But we're not Bigfoot's love child," I said as we all laughed. "I know it's too cold to play Frisbee outside, but how come we can't use the armory?"

"The major had the new commander collect everyone's keys, so I don't have access anymore," Jesse said.

Tim took a bite of his hotdog. "Is everyone up there satisfied with how the murder case was closed?"

"Yeah, most of the guardsmen thought Sergeant Inversol was a grouch and weren't sorry to see him go. As his assistant, I worked with him all the time and came to like him. It wasn't easy. He was a loner and didn't want to sit around and shoot the bull, but as long as you left him alone and did your job, he treated you fairly. As for the colonel, nobody liked that pint-size Napoleon wannabe. We are all hoping for a pushover replacement. The temporary guy is just marking time till he can escape," Jesse said as he inhaled another wiener.

I took a drink of my lemon Coke. "Well, I'm not buying the case-closed line. It just doesn't add up. It's like we have only the four corner pieces to a one-hundred-piece jigsaw puzzle and everyone is telling us how pretty the picture is."

"Katie's not buying it either," Tim added. "She is sure Inversol didn't kill her dad, and she wants to find out who did. We are sitting on some explosive evidence that raises questions about the sergeant's guilt, and we need to figure out what we're going to do with it. Can't we give it to the police or the Army?"

"No and no," I said. "The Army has washed their hands of this mess, and the chief of police is one of the photogenic subjects of the black-and-white glossies you want to share. And what about the pain those photos will cause Katie? She's already lost her dad and friend. If those get out, her mom will have to leave town."

"Yeah, you're right, but we've got to do something," Tim said.

Jesse tapped the table with his drink glass. "Let's see if we can find some more pieces to that puzzle on our own. All we've got so far is a bunch of sex pics, and there isn't anything in them that proves Inversol didn't kill the colonel and then himself. What else do we have?"

"We know that Inversol was a drug addict and needed money to maintain his habit," Tim said.

I pushed Tim with my shoulder. "Right, but where was he getting the morphine? He told Katie his supplier knew how to sew up his bullet wound, and that's not something you learn in Boy Scouts."

"And hospitals have to report gunshot wounds," Tim added.

Jesse pursed his lips. "But veterinarians don't. They have access to morphine just like your dad, and there must be three or four of them in town."

"It's still a schedule two drug, which means whoever has it has to account for every drop used. My dad told me that," Tim said while trying not to look like a know-it-all.

Chapter Sixteen - Puzzle Pieces

I took a bite of my hotdog and chewed it thoroughly. "Well, someone in town has got to know who sells morphine on the side, or Jack wouldn't have found out about it."

Mr. Giatras stopped at our table and asked, "You boys want another wiener?"

I hadn't finished my first one, and Tim was only halfway through his second.

"Absolutely," said Jesse. "Two more for me."

I waited for our host to leave then asked, "Jesse, would the guy you get your weed from know where to buy drugs like that?"

"Shit if I know. It's a pretty big jump from Maui wowie to morphine."

Tim cleared his throat. "Actually, marijuana is a schedule one drug. The government considers it more dangerous than medical opiates."

We both stared at Tim, a bit amazed.

"Well, I guess I can ask," Jesse said as Mr. Giatras set a paper plate with two steaming wieners down in front of him. "But I have to be careful with this guy; he's going to want to know why I'm asking. You may know drugs, Tim, but I know how to eat wieners," Jesse said as he lifted the two dogs at once and bit the ends off both of them.

I grabbed my half-eaten wiener and shook it at Jesse. "Okay then, ask."

Chapter Seventeen
Checkup

Three days later, I got a call from Jesse, and he was pumped.

"I'll pick you up tonight at nine thirty. We've got to be at Ferdinand's by ten—sharp."

"Okay, why?"

"I know who Inversol's supplier is, and I'm to meet him there. Have you got a tape recorder?"

"Yeah, a cassette one, but it needs new batteries."

"Buy them and bring it with you tonight." Jesse hung up.

I was ready to go and had my Panasonic tape recorder, with its new batteries, neatly stashed in my gym bag when Jesse pulled up in front of my house in an old Rambler. I wasn't sure it was him until he beeped the horn and waved.

I plopped down onto the pillow-soft cloth-covered seat, looked at Jesse, and said laughingly, "Now this is one stylish ride. I bet you get some serious leg in this."

Jesse gave me a stern look. "Do not give me any shit. It's my old man's car. My VW's battery is still dead, and I can't spare the cash to replace it if I'm buying morphine tonight."

"We're buying morphine?" I asked, hoping the answer was no.

"I'm not sure, but I'm ready if I need to. Two days ago, I talked with my weed dealer and asked him if he knew where

Chapter Seventeen - Checkup

I could get some painkillers. I told him I had an opportunity to make some serious money if I could get my hands on a steady supply of morphine. I let him believe that I knew Sergeant Inversol was sharing his stash with other so-inclined guardsmen and the demand was still there. All I needed to do was provide the supply. He said he could put his hands on some horse tranquilizers, but that was it. I pushed him a bit more, but he was hesitant to share anything else until I told him I'd give him a ten-percent cut of whatever I made."

"Greed conquers all," I said.

Jesse chuckled. "For sure. He then told me about a dentist named Barry Huntler who may be able to help me, but he had to talk to him first."

"A dentist?" I asked. "I thought we were looking for a veterinarian?"

"So did I. But yesterday morning, my dealer called me and said I had an appointment with Doctor Huntler at five. I showed up there and checked in with the receptionist and waited. Five o'clock came and went, and so did the receptionist. Then at five twenty, this chubby guy in a white lab coat sticks his head into the waiting room and says, 'Next.' Well, I was the only one there, so I went in, and it got weird."

I set my gym bag on the seat beside me. "What do you mean?"

"He played dumb. I asked him if he knew why I was there, and he said, 'Yes. You're new in town and need a dentist.' I told him that was only part of it and was about to mention the morphine when he stopped me and said, 'Sit down and let's see how your teeth look.' I went along, and he gave me a routine checkup—teeth cleaning and all. When it was over, he told me I had a nasty cavity in my thirty-first molar."

I laughed and pointed at my teeth. "Look, Mom, no cavities."

"Shut up," Jesse said. "I thought my dealer had played a joke on me with this guy and said, 'Hey, Doc, I didn't come here to get a filling; I need something to take away the pain.' That got a response. The dentist put his hand up and said, 'Not here and not now. I've got a call into a friend at the National Guard headquarters, checking you out. I was hoping to have heard back from him by now but haven't. That's why we started late. Can you meet me tonight? If I show up, the call was positive. If I don't, you may not want to go back to your Army job.' And that's why we're on our way to Ferdinand's. Oh, and you know that S.O.B. charged me ten bucks for the checkup."

"Great, what do you want me to do?" I asked.

"Have you got your tape recorder?"

I patted the gym bag. "Right here."

"Good, get in the trunk and be ready to record. Your signal to start will be when I turn off the music. Whatever you do, be quiet," Jesse said.

"You're kidding me. We're going to a fast food joint, not a drive-in theater," I protested.

"Look, I need you to record whatever this guy says, and he can't see you doing it, so you're going to do it from the trunk.

Chapter Seventeen - Checkup

If he agrees to sell me morphine, I want it on tape just in case he gets cold feet and threatens to turn me in as a weed dealer." Jesse pulled over to the side of the road, opened his door, and walked to the back of the car.

I wasn't happy, but I climbed into the trunk and curled myself into a position that would allow me to hold the microphone up to the cardboard shelf behind the back seat. The trunk floor was hard and uneven, and everything smelled of spare tire. Jesse slammed the lid then knocked twice on top.

"S'all right?"

"S'all right," I answered.

I heard Jesse start the car and then slide a tape into the under-dash player. There was a loud click as the tape advanced to the next track. Then Dean Martin crooned "Everybody Loves Somebody Sometime."

"Thank God, we're only a mile from Ferdinand's," I said out loud.

"Shut up, I can hear you!" Jesse yelled.

Ferdinand's was an old-style drive-in restaurant with parking spaces equipped with two-way radios so you could order food and eat in your car. I knew we were there when colored neon light flooded in through the seams of the car's trunk. As Jesse killed the engine, I got my tape recorder ready. Dean was in the middle of "Volare" when Jesse pulled the tape out of the machine, and I heard the back door open. Someone got in.

"Let's go for a drive," an unfamiliar voice said, and I heard Jesse grunt his agreement and start the engine. We bounced over a curb-cut roughly, and it lifted me off the floor of the trunk. I hit the lid hard. The trunk popped open and swung up out of reach.

The back seat passenger said, "Your trunk is open," and Jesse slammed on the brakes. This threw me forward like a bag of rocks, and I hit the back side of the back seat with a thud.

"What the hell do you have in the trunk? It sounds like a dead body rolling around in there," carped the passenger.

Jesse opened his door. "It's my Army duffle bag. I have to keep it with me at all times in case I'm called up."

The passenger opened his door, too. "I'll close it for you."

"No! I've got it," said Jesse.

Reaching up, I was able to grab the lid and was pulling it down slowly when Jesse's strong arms slammed it shut, hitting my head.

Both doors closed, and Jesse drove on. In the minute it took me to reorient myself and get the microphone in place, the conversation began. I pushed the record button.

"But, Doctor, I'm ready if you are—"

Dr. Huntler interrupted Jesse. "Just because I know you're in the National Guard doesn't mean I trust you."

"Okay, but don't you want to make money?" Jesse asked.

"What's your offer?"

Chapter Seventeen - Checkup

"Continuity. I'm offering you continuity of sales. I'm the guy who can maintain the cash flow you were getting from Sergeant Inversol."

"Go on," Huntler said.

"I know the product. I was Inversol's bagman. He'd get the stuff from you, keep half of it for himself, then pass the rest to me to distribute to the guys at the armory. I'd collect the cash, take my cut, and return the rest to the sergeant. If you work with me, you eliminate the middleman, and I can move more product for you, generating more cash."

I heard Huntler shift in his seat. "How much product? Inversol's death left me holding a lot."

"Oh, really?" Jesse asked. "I thought he was just getting a few bottles a month."

"He was, but just before he died, he asked me to get fifteen bottles for him, and I did. Can you move that many?"

"Yes, I can. It might take me a while to put that much cash together, but I can take that off your hands," Jesse assured the doctor.

There was a long pause before Huntler replied. "I knew Inversol; I don't know you. That means more risk for me, and so you're not going to get his deal. I want two hundred and twenty dollars a bottle, not two hundred."

"Two hundred and five; and I'll take five bottles off your hands in two weeks, three more next month, and a minimum of three every month forward."

There was another long pause before Huntler said, "Two hundred and ten."

"Deal," said Jesse.

"Deal," said Huntler. "Make sure you bring cash. Christmas is coming, and my wife wants a new Buick." Huntler laughed loudly, and Jesse joined him. "The dealer has a baby-blue Riviera waiting for me."

"I'll have your down payment next week. I promise," said Jesse.

"You damn well better. If that woman doesn't get a Riviera, I'll need a chiropractor."

There was more laughter as we bumped back over the curb-cut, and my metal tomb was bathed in neon light again. The rear car door opened and closed, and then Jesse backed out of the parking lot. This time, he only drove about a block before pulling off the main road.

Jesse opened the trunk. "Did you get it?"

"Every word, but I feel like a sock that just finished the spin cycle in a washing machine."

"Come on. You can tumble dry in the front seat. I've got the heater on high. We learned a lot, didn't we?" Jesse asked.

I crawled out of the trunk. "Yes, but I have more questions now than before."

Chapter Seventeen - Checkup

"Really? We know where the morphine was coming from, and we have an incriminating tape recording just in case," Jesse said.

"Right, but what's with this fifteen-bottle order? Where in the world was the sergeant going to come up with the three thousand dollars for fifteen bottles, and why did he want them all at once?" I asked. "The man didn't have three dollars to spare; he was living at the YMCA, for Christ's sake."

"Yeah," said Jesse, realizing that the new puzzle pieces we had didn't fit with the others.

I shook my head. "And another thing. Even if he was blackmailing Colonel Bandershot for the two hundred a month, there is no way Bandershot could have come up with three thousand dollars. He was broke. And if Inversol died before paying the dentist, where's the three thousand dollars?"

Jesse looked at me. "Hey, wait. How do you know Bandershot was broke?"

I smiled. "I'll tell you on the way to Pop Snyder's. This duffle bag needs a drink."

Chapter Eighteen
Jack's Office

The egg-shaped, dishwasher-sized BMW Isetta minicar rolled up beside me and opened its mouth of a front door. Out tumbled a clown, two Shriners, a goat, and a dwarf. The dwarf was dressed as one of Santa's elves. He had spent the last hour sitting on top of the car waving to kids while the Shriners and the clown ran circles around it yelling, "Chinese fire drill!" and squirting seltzer water at each other. I don't know what the goat did, but someone had duct-taped plastic reindeer antlers to its horns, and it was now trying to rub them off on a lamp post.

The annual Cumberland downtown Christmas parade was over, and the streets were clearing quickly, but the Shriners needed to get their cars back to the garage. The Isetta was only one of a fleet of small cars the Shriners had at the parade. As I watched, a flatbed truck pulled up, and men prepared the car for loading.

I looked a bit odd as well; I was still wearing my drum major uniform and carrying my eighteen-inch busby hat under my arm. The band had finished marching thirty minutes earlier, and most of the members had scattered to get in out of the cold, but I was stuck in front of the YMCA waiting for Tim and Katie to get the car.

The BMW was being strapped down as Katie drove up in her mom's Eldorado. The two cars both held four people, but

Chapter Eighteen - Jack's Office

that's where the similarities stopped. You could put the Isetta in the Eldorado's trunk and still have room for golf clubs.

I bent over as Katie's power window slid down. "Get in."

Tim opened the passenger door and tilted the thick front seat forward. I fell into a couch-sized leather-clad back seat and found myself watching the dwarf walk off with the goat through a narrow opera window. Katie hit the gas, and our twenty feet of conspicuous American consumption lurched forward.

Katie was a binary driver. She had only two modes: accelerate or brake. We were in accelerate mode as we raced to her house so she could change out of her skintight, sequin-covered twirler's uniform.

"Does your mom know you have her car tonight?" I asked.

"Yes, she's out with Don."

"Who's Don?" I asked, hoping it was the guy Mrs. Bandershot was with on the porch. Tim looked back at me and gave me a quick nod.

Katie shifted into mode two and slammed on the brakes to avoid running a red light. "He's an old friend who has been helping Mom with everything since Dad died. He just survived an ugly divorce that ended with his wife leaving town with his two kids. It was Don's idea we go to Massachusetts, and although I was trapped at my uncle's house watching TV for two weeks, I think it calmed Mom down."

I bounced off Tim's seat back and looked around for help. "Hey, are there seat belts back here?" I asked as the light turned green and Katie's foot pushed the accelerator to the floor again.

"No, Mom thinks they mar the beauty of the leather, so she had them removed."

Pinned to the back seat, I grabbed the armrest to reduce my bouncing around. "What does Don do?"

"He's a Kelly Springfield man. I think VP for regional distribution or something like that," Katie said.

"Where's he from?" Tim asked.

"I'm not sure. Illinois, maybe. I do know he was a big wig in a college fraternity out there; every year he goes to their reunion.

Tim looked at me and silently mouthed, "Fraternity."

"Hey, Tim said you don't think Jack's case should have been closed," Katie said as she swerved to avoid hitting a car attempting to parallel park.

"Katie, I just don't buy Inversol as a killer."

"Exactly!" Katie said. "Jack was a sweetie pie. Mom couldn't stand him, but I loved him."

"Why didn't your mom like Jack?" Tim asked.

"Well, Mom knew about his problems, and she told me Jack asked Dad for some money once. I guess it was a loan or something, but she shut it down. Anyway, we need to clear Jack's name. What can we do?"

Our speed had leveled out at twice the limit, and I felt comfortable enough to let go of the armrest. "You know, the

Chapter Eighteen - Jack's Office

case is closed, so there isn't any reason why we can't snoop around a little and see if we can find out something new."

"Perfect," Katie said as she turned into her driveway and skidded to a halt. "You guys wait in the foyer while I change."

"Need any help?" Tim offered.

Katie's look made it clear that Tim was to stay downstairs.

You could have parked two Eldorados in Katie's foyer. Huge mirrors hung on the side walls, and there was a life-sized portrait of her mom at the top of the Carrara marble staircase. Even in oil, Pat Bandershot was menacing.

It wasn't more than ten minutes before Katie came bounding down the stairs. "I've got an idea. Let's search Jack's office and see what we can find."

"We can't get into the armory anymore. They took Jesse's keys away from him," Tim said.

Katie twirled a small ring of keys around her finger. "No problem, I made a copy of Dad's set long ago. I used them to visit Jack without Dad knowing. How do you think I got that record player out of his office when we were dancing at the armory?"

"Maybe we should look in your dad's armory office as well," Tim added.

"Nope, Mom and Don cleared that out a couple of days after the case was closed. They stored everything away except his record player and march music LPs. Mom hates marches, and the Guard can use them for drill practice."

Katie drove Tim and me home so we could change. Then we went straight to the armory. It was close to eight o'clock when she slid the Eldorado into the commander's parking space.

I had my flashlight with me but kept it off until we were inside.

"Which one's Jack's office?" I asked.

Katie turned down the long hallway on the left. "This way."

"Hey, don't the offices have individual keys?" Tim asked.

Katie unlocked the door to Sergeant Inversol's office. "Yes, they do, but Dad's is a master key. It opens up every lock in this place except the iron-barred door to the bunker."

I flipped on my flashlight, and we saw Jack's desktop and drawers were empty. The bookcase behind the desk was also empty. All the sergeant's belongings were in cardboard boxes scattered about the floor.

"Looks like we are just in time. They're getting ready to put Jack's stuff in storage," Katie said.

I looked down at the flashlight and then all the boxes. "There is no way we are going to be able to go through all of these with only one flashlight."

Katie ordered Tim to close the window blinds, and then she turned on the overhead light. "Shelby, you take the boxes by the wall, and I'll do these behind the desk. Tim, you do the rest of them."

"Yes, sir," Tim barked. "You sure have your dad's commanding personality."

Katie stuck her tongue out.

Chapter Eighteen - Jack's Office

With the lights on, we went to work.

I was opening my second of three boxes when I heard voices outside. The main door to the armory opened, and the voices got louder. Tim jumped up and flipped the lights off, and we huddled together, not sure what to do.

The lights in the gym went on, and the sound of heavy things being moved around echoed down the hall. Jack's office was bathed in a soft glow as light trickled in from the gym. I could see my partners in crime as we hunched down among the boxes.

"What now?" Tim whispered.

"Did either of you find anything?" I asked.

Katie held up some papers. "I've got Jack's desk calendar and some handwritten notes that look interesting."

"All I have is a box of receipts," Tim said.

I was about to say I hadn't found anything when footsteps fell on the polished concrete floors of the hallway. A shadow passed our door, paused, and then continued. We froze solid as a tongue on a flagpole in January. Then we heard a door open and close down the hall, and the shadow was gone.

I raised my head enough to look out the door's window. "Let's sit tight for a minute."

Tim and Katie nodded, and we listened as the men busied themselves in the gym. We heard a thud as something heavy hit the floor then the noise of rolling and pulling. Then the sounds changed. We heard balls bouncing off rackets and sneakers squeaking on the floor.

I put my finger up to my lips then my hands up in a stopping motion, signaling to Tim and Katie to keep quiet and not move. Opening the office door, I walked into the hall. Light poured out of the side door of the gym as I peeked in. There I saw four men in white shorts and shirts playing tennis on an improvised indoor court. The court was made of long strips of rubber matting less than a quarter of an inch thick. The net was held in place by two weighted poles, and if I hadn't known better, I'd have thought I was watching a doubles match on a warm summer day at the country club.

I crept back to Jack's office and told Tim and Katie what I saw.

Katie giggled. "Oh, gosh, I forgot all about that. It's the Cumberland Men's Tennis Association's winter league. They rent the armory a few times a month and roll out their indoor tennis court."

"Cool," Tim said.

Katie peeked out the door. "Yeah, I've played on it once, and it's just like playing outdoors. Don's a member."

I nodded towards the hallway. "Okay, grab whatever you think is important, and let's slip out the side door. I think our Wimbledon friends are distracted enough not to notice us."

We snuck down the hall and out the door without being seen.

Well, at least we thought so.

Chapter Nineteen
Burn Them

Friday was the last day of school before the Christmas holiday, and classes were a big nothing. The teachers were just going through the motions, knowing the students had already checked out. In Latin, Bruce Baker read to us from *The Magic Christian* by Terry Southern, a comic novel about a billionaire who stages elaborate practical jokes. In one, he tricks people into pulling money out of a heated concrete bowl full of manure.

I loved Latin class.

My locker was just down the hall, and I found Katie and Tim waiting for me there.

"Mom wants you all to come to our house for dinner tonight, and by all, I mean Jesse, too," Katie said.

"Why?" I asked.

"She wants to get to know the people I have been hanging out with recently. Trust me on this; we can't resist her. If you guys don't show up, she'll ban me from seeing you."

Tim looked worried. He had the most to lose. "Do you think you can get Jesse to come?"

"I'll try," I said. "He is usually working at the church this time of day."

Tim grabbed my arm. "Let's drive over there now."

Katie waved as we walked down the hall. "Don't get to my place before six. Mom starts drinking at lunch, but she doesn't hit the hard stuff until five, and I want her well lubricated before you guys show up."

Tim and I drove to the church, and we found Jesse replacing burned-out Christmas lights that hung over the nativity scene on the front lawn.

Jesse looked up from his work. "There are over two hundred lights out here, and at least five of them burn out every day."

"Crappy job, but someone has to maintain this perfect replica of Jesus's birthplace as we approach his one thousand nine hundred and seventy-second birthday," I said.

Tim put his hands together in prayer. "And, lo, the angel of the Lord came upon them, and the glory of the Lord shone round about them, and they were sore afraid for they had not yet put up their Christmas lights. Luke 2:9."

Jesse shook his head. "That's bent."

"Thank you," said Tim.

Jesse agreed to go with us to Katie's but said he had something he needed to show us first. We followed him to his VW bus, and he got a piece of paper out of the glove box.

"Check this out; my dad got it at the police station. It's a copy of the evidence list from Bandershot's murder case. I asked him to keep an eye open for information, and last night, Chief Tompkins had his secretary make a copy of the entire Bandershot file. It seems the mayor has taken a personal

Chapter Nineteen - Burn Them

interest in the case. The secretary made some mistakes while copying and threw the bad ones away. Dad got them out of the trash, and the evidence list was one of them."

"Anything interesting?" I asked.

"Maybe. Check out item number twelve. An EOD report from October the police found in Sergeant Inversol's office," Jesse said.

Tim took the paper from Jesse. "What's EOD?"

"Explosive ordnance disposal. They're the team that comes in from DC after we've had a live-fire exercise. There's a restricted firing range out by the Super-51 drive-in where we do all our live ammunition training, and each time we finish, an EOD team goes in there and makes sure we didn't leave any live ammunition lying around."

"So what?" I asked.

"I checked the logbook, and we haven't had a live-fire exercise in over a year, so why is there an EOD team report from two months ago? Hey, I've got to get back to work. How about you pick me up at five forty-five for our Cruella de Vil dinner party. I still haven't replaced the battery in my bus, but I got it recharged, and I don't want to overtax it. Oh, and please tell me I don't have to wear a tux with tails?"

Tim got a serious look on his face. "No tux, but Mrs. Bandershot gets hives if you wear blue jeans around her."

"Do you have a copy of the EOD report?" I asked Jesse.

"Nope, only the list, but there should be one in the files at the armory."

I pointed at my car. "We've got some stuff from Inversol's office we need to go through. It's in the trunk under the carpet with the spare tire. I hid the photos there, too."

"Shit, man, I told you I don't want to know where those naked pictures are," Jesse scolded. "And how in the hell did you get into the sergeant's office?"

"Sorry, I forgot. Katie has a set of her old man's master keys. We can get into anything we want up there," I said.

"You white folk are nothing but trouble," Jesse said and returned to his work.

We arrived at Palace Bandershot at precisely six o'clock and knocked on the elaborate art nouveau front doors. Katie greeted us with a stricken look on her face. "There's no dinner. We've been ambushed."

"Come in, gentlemen," said a man's familiar voice. Katie stepped back, and we entered. Standing in the doorway to the living room was a thin man about five-foot-ten with dark hair pasted tightly to the side of his head with some kind of product. From the way it glistened, my guess would be it was Wildroot. His face was pinched and taut—more ferret than fox.

"My name's Dickerson, Don Dickerson. Please join us," he said, turning back into the living room and gesturing for us to follow.

Chapter Nineteen - Burn Them

Jesse bumped me with his arm. "This is what I was afraid of. It doesn't matter who did what. They're going to pin the shit on the black man."

I couldn't tell if he was afraid or preparing for a fight. We followed Dickerson into the living room.

Lounging in a high-backed armchair in front of a roaring fireplace was Pat Bandershot with a drink in one hand and a cigarette holder in the other. Smoke weaved its way up from the cigarette's tip and blossomed near the twenty-foot-high ceiling. She was dressed in a white pantsuit with oversized Captain Kangaroo pockets outlined in green. Her face was a mask of anger.

"You know the chief, of course," she said, tilting her head to the right as she took a long drag on her cigarette and stood.

That's when I knew we were in trouble, for standing at the far end of the room near a fully stocked bar was Cumberland's Chief of Police Thompkins, in uniform. He lifted his tumbler full of ice and scotch in our direction and smiled as light glinted from his star-spangled lapels.

My sphincter clenched tighter than a hangman's noose after a six-foot drop. I pulled my collar away from my neck for some air.

The adults moved in our direction and formed a firing squad around us.

Don Dickerson fired first. "I saw the Eldorado at the armory last night, Katie, so there is no use denying that it was you and your friends rummaging around in Sergeant Inversol's office."

"What were you looking for?" Pat Bandershot said sharply. "More pictures?"

"It would be best if you tell us the truth. If you don't, your situation will only get worse," Chief Thompkins added.

Katie stamped her foot. "What are you talking about, Mother?"

"Don't be cute with me, Katherine. The pictures, the key club pictures. We know Inversol had a copy of them. He was using them to blackmail your father, threatening to give them to the newspaper, but now, his copies are missing."

Chief Thompkins used his finger to stir his drink. "That's right. I searched Inversol's room at the YMCA and couldn't find them, and they weren't in his office when the police arrived after his death."

Pat Bandershot took over the grilling. "The only person there before the police was your jolly black giant over here, so that means you and your friends must have the pictures."

I could feel Jesse's muscles tense as he shifted his stance into a defensive crouch.

"Easy, boy," Chief Thompkins said curtly as he moved his right hand to his holster.

"What pictures?" Katie pleaded. "We don't have any pictures."

"Yes, we do," said Tim. "I'm sorry, Katie. You just haven't seen them, and you shouldn't."

Chapter Nineteen - Burn Them

Katie's face went blank as she looked first at Tim then Jesse then me.

Mrs. Bandershot sat back down stunned by the realization she had just exposed her secret to her daughter, not us.

"Where are they?" Don Dickerson yelled, moving up behind Tim and spinning him around by the shoulder.

"What's in it for us?" I asked, trying to sound confident while I felt as if my legs were made of Jell-O.

"Why you little—" Dickerson said, shifting in my direction but maintaining his volume. "I have destroyed every photo that man took and his negatives too, except for the ones the sergeant was using for blackmail. Give them to me now!" he screamed into my face.

I felt his spittle on my forehead as I ducked, avoiding a collision. "Only if you and Chief Thompkins assure me that nothing comes of this. It ends here, and no one, not Katie, Tim, Jesse, or I suffer any consequences."

"That's right," said Jesse as he stepped to my side and pushed Dickerson back as easily as he would push a pillow off a couch.

Smoothing his Wildroot-drenched hair, Dickerson backed off. He had no choice. Jesse was at least two weight classes above him.

"Okay, let's calm this down a bit," said Police Chief Thompkins, looking at me. "If you give us the photos, not a word will be said about this going forward. Do we have a deal?"

Slippery When Wet

Katie had dropped to the floor at her mother's feet and was staring at her blankly.

"Okay," I answered. "Wait here." I turned to leave, but Dickerson blocked my way.

"Where are you going?"

"To my car. The photos are there." I brushed past him and walked out of the room.

I returned with the manila envelope that had been in the car ever since my visit to the library with Tim. I held it tightly, knowing it was our one ticket out of this mess.

Mrs. Bandershot was up again and came over to me with her hand out. "Give them to me—now."

I looked at Tim and Jesse, and they both nodded. Then I looked down at the manila envelope. My hands were trembling as I handed them to her.

Pat Bandershot turned away and walked towards the other end of the room as she fumbled with the envelope's clasp. Freeing it, she removed the photos and flipped through them quickly.

"There's one missing," she announced as she returned the images and walked over to Dickerson.

"Which one?" Dickerson asked.

She handed them to him. "Burn them."

Chapter Nineteen - Burn Them

Dickerson opened the envelope and pulled the pictures halfway out. He looked at the chief and shook his head before he let them fall back. Then he walked towards the fireplace.

As Dickerson crossed in front of Katie, she thrust herself up like a geyser and grabbed for the envelope. Dickerson was knocked back but held tight to his prize. Then the unthinkable happened: the envelope tore open, and the photos fluttered onto Pat Bandershot's beautiful Persian rug. We were all treated to the same collage I had first seen on Jesse's microbus floor.

All the oxygen was sucked out of the room as everyone's focus shifted to the glossy black-and-white photos.

"No!" Pat Bandershot screamed and dropped to the floor, trying to cover with her body the photos of her uncovered body.

She was too late. Katie had snatched one up and was studying it as she walked away from her mother. It was the photo with the gynecologist, the worst of the bunch.

Realizing the futility of her situation, Pat Bandershot sat up, straightened her blouse, and began to pick up the remaining five pictures one at a time and toss them into the fireplace.

Katie returned to her mother's side and knelt.

"Sorry, Mommy," she said as she handed the sixth photo to her.

Their tear-filled eyes met as Pat took the photo and threw it into the fire.

Katie and her mother exited the room quickly, and I hoped the intensity of the final minutes of the evening would subside.

"Get out!" Dickerson yelled at us. "Get the hell out of this house."

"Chief, do we still have a deal?" Jesse asked.

Thompkins looked at Dickerson and got a nod. "Yes, we'll say nothing if you say nothing. Now leave."

Tim, Jesse, and I walked to my car, knowing we had just survived a near miss, and the thing that missed us was a trainload of hurt.

After the doors closed, we all sat quietly for a while.

I was the first to speak. "I guess that's the end of that."

Tim added, "Yeah, I guess."

Jesse started to say something then stopped, sat briefly in silence, and then tried again. "Hey, wait, this isn't the end of anything. We're right where we started."

"What do you mean?" Tim asked.

"We still don't know if Sergeant Inversol killed the colonel or if he killed himself," Jesse said. "There could be a murderer walking around out there scot-free, and no one is doing a damn thing about it. Mrs. Bandershot, Dickerson, and the chief are happy. They got what they wanted—the photos—but we got diddly-squat."

Chapter Nineteen - Burn Them

The power of Jesse's words increased. "Listen, you know I'm not happy about being the only black dude in this shit pile. I thought the way out was to stay out of it, but that's not working. So, I'm in, and I tell you what, guys. I want to know what happened to Sergeant Inversol."

Tim jumped in. "We did find out the sergeant was blackmailing his boss."

"Well, that's true," I said. "I guess that's where his morphine money was coming from, but I still don't understand what Inversol was doing with the photos on his desk when he died. And what was that Katie's mom said about a missing photo?"

Jesse hit the back of my seat. "We don't know bupkis."

If we weren't so exhausted, Tim and I might have responded with more enthusiasm, but all we could muster was "Yeah."

The drive to Jesse's house was quiet, but as he got out of the car, I said, "Listen, Jesse, you're right. Let's get to the bottom of this pile of shit and then go find out who dumped it on us."

"Agree," said Tim. "We need to go over the stuff we got out of Inversol's office. There has got to be something there that will point us in the right direction."

Jesse held up a clenched fist. "Right on. When do we start?"

I gave him a thumbs-up. "Tomorrow may be Christmas Eve, but it's a work day for us. Be at my house at ten, and we'll figure this out."

Chapter Twenty
Clues

Everything was laid out on the pool table: the copy of the suicide note, the receipts and calendar we found in Sergeant Inversol's office, and the case evidence list Jesse's father got from the police station. There were about twenty items in total.

"There's not that much for us to work with," said Jesse.

I closed my eyes and waved my hand over the pool table like a magician. "The answers are here. We can see the iron filings moving. All we need to do is find out who's holding the magnet." I opened my eyes. "Let's start with each of us looking over everything. Then we'll compare notes."

It was five after ten in the morning on Christmas Eve, and we were gathered in my basement scrutinizing the chicken scratches of Jack Inversol.

After forty minutes, I said, "Merry Christmas. I'm finished; how about you?"

"Happy New Year," Tim said. "I'm done too. Did you find anything, Jesse?"

"Give me a minute. I think I've found something important on the calendar."

"Take your time. Tim. Let's get a Coke. Jesse, do you want one?" I asked.

"No thanks."

Chapter Twenty - Clues

When we returned, Jesse was sitting on the pool table dangling his feet off the side. "I may have something that ties a couple of things together."

"What?" Tim asked.

Jesse picked up the notebook-style five-year calendar and flipped through it. "There's an entry here that reads 'Don Pit 3:30 p.m.' on the fifteenth of September."

He handed it to me. "Yeah, I saw that, but who is Don Pit, and what's so special about him? There are at least ten other names in that calendar."

Jesse tapped his finger on the date. "I know, but I recognized all the other names as either members of our unit or people Inversol regularly met with. I've never heard of a Don Pit."

I looked at the date again. "So, what's so special about the sergeant meeting with a guy you don't know named Don Pit?"

"I don't think it's a who; I think it's a what," Jesse said. "Well, half of it's a what. That place near the Super-51 where we do our live ammunition testing; we call it The Pit. The area is dug into a hillside so the firing is contained. If you miss the target, your bullet just slams into the dirt. It kind of looks like a pit, and that's how it got its name."

"Shit," I heard myself say. "Do you think the Don on the calendar is that greasy weasel Don Dickerson, and they met at this pit place?"

"Maybe," Jesse said, "That's the only Don who has anything to do with this mess, but we better be careful. There are a lot of Dons in Cumberland, and one of them might have the last name Pit."

"But what would Don Dickerson be doing with Inversol at a firing range?" I asked.

Tim took the calendar. "Beats me. Katie told me Don is anything but a gun guy. He's more tennis and hot toddies than tanks."

"It doesn't matter. It's against Guard policy to take civilians to The Pit," Jesse said. "There are plenty of public firing ranges around here they could have used. Guns are big business in Cumberland."

I sorted through the pile of papers on the pool table. "Unless you want to use a weapon you can't use anywhere else."

I found the evidence list and held it up. "The kind of weapon you would need an explosive ordnance disposal team to come in and clean up after you."

"Grenades," Jesse said.

"Grenades," Tim said softly. "Could Don Dickerson be Colonel Bandershot's killer?" His voice got quiet for a second then came back stronger. "The dates match up. Dickerson and Inversol go to The Pit on September fifteenth, the EOD team writes their report in October, and the colonel is blown to bits a month later."

Chapter Twenty - Clues

Tim paused again, looked down like he was trying to remember a name, then said, "And Dickerson is a frat boy. Katie told us so the other night."

"Maybe Delta Phi," I said.

Jesse took the evidence list from my hand. "We need to see that EOD report."

I nodded. "Yes, we do, and we should wait until we see it to speculate any further."

"Right, but that's a damn big clue. Did either of you find anything like it?" Jesse asked.

"Not really, but there was a math problem on the back of one of the receipts that didn't make any sense. Did you see it?" Tim asked.

Jesse moved next to Tim. "Which receipt?"

Tim picked up a small piece of paper from the table. "This one."

It was from Parkview Liquors. On the front of it was recorded the sale of two pints of Jack Daniel's on October fifth. On the back was what looked like an addition problem. At the top were two numbers separated by a minus sign: 10 - 16. Underneath those numbers was 30M and underneath that was 20C. Then there was a straight line and finally in the position of the sum was 10K.

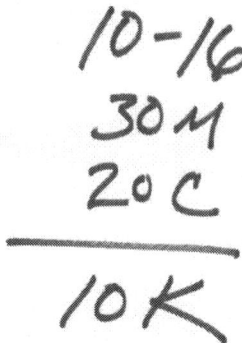

Tim passed the receipt to me, and after looking it over, I gave it to Jesse.

"Parkview Liquors," Jesse laughed. "Hell, Inversol bought booze at Parkview Liquors every day. He needed two pints of Jack Daniel's on board just to function. The only thing holding him back from drinking more was being able to pay for it."

"So why did he save this receipt?" I asked. "It's the only one from Parkview. All the others are work-related even the receipt from the dry cleaners for his uniform. This math problem on the back must have been important to him."

Tim shook the receipt in his hand. "But it doesn't add up. I mean that's not a regular addition or subtraction problem unless the sergeant was versed in Roman numerals. I think the Roman numeral C stands for one hundred and M for fifty."

Chapter Twenty - Clues

"One thousand, M is for *mille* which is one thousand in Latin," I said, laughing. "Wow, I remembered something from Latin class other than that crazy stuff in *The Magic Christian*."

"Okay, Cicero, what's K stand for?" Tim asked.

I thought for a second but couldn't remember any Roman numeral K.

Tim pointed to the receipt. "Speaking of numbers and Parkview Liquors, we never found out who Ed was,"

"Ed who?" Jesse asked.

"Ed, the guy whose name was beside Parkview's phone number on the back of one of the original photos," Tim explained.

"It's probably just Jack's favorite Parkview Liquors peddler," I said.

Jesse had the calendar again and was leafing through it. "Enough with the numbers. All this talk about Parkview reminds me of something else I found in the calendar, near the end of the year, I think. Yes, here it is on New Year's Eve. There's an entry reading 'Parkview Pickup' with no time listed."

I took the calendar from Jesse. "Well, that could be just a reminder for the sergeant to buy his nerve medicine."

"No, I don't think so, I told you he bought a couple of pints of booze there every day. I think it was one of his daily rituals, like shaving," Jesse said. "He didn't write anything about shaving in his calendar, so why would he need one for buying his Jack Daniel's and why is there only one entry on that date?"

"Maybe he was making a big purchase for a New Year's Eve party," Tim offered.

"Maybe, but it's strange," Jesse said.

I interrupted. "Okay, is there anything else?"

Both Tim and Jesse were silent.

I started to pick up the papers from the pool table. "My mom and dad will be home soon, and I have to get all this stuff put away before they get here.

Tim helped me. "We need to see the EOD report."

Jesse pushed me from behind. "So, let's go get it."

Chapter Twenty-One
The Report

The clock radio said I had an hour and a half before the midnight church service, but I also had all my presents to wrap. On my bed were the things I'd bought for my family, but I hadn't wrapped any of them. I hated wrapping gifts.

Mom cracked open my bedroom door. "What are you doing, honey? Come on downstairs and sing some Christmas carols with us. Dad's got his trumpet out, and we're ready to make some music."

"Hey, no peeking. I've got presents in here," I said while covering up the bottle of perfume that was her gift.

The doorbell rang, and I dashed out of my room, pushing past Mom and forgetting all about the presents.

It was Tim and Katie. "Here you go," Katie said as she handed me her keys to the armory.

Tim was holding Katie's hand. "We just came from my church's Christmas Eve service. Katie didn't want to be with her mom and Don at the Episcopal one."

I put the keys in my pocket. "Good idea. Stay as far away from Dickerson as you can until we know if he's dirty. Where are you going now?"

"My place," Tim said. "Call as soon as you've seen the report."

"Okay." I went to join my family playing Christmas music.

Jesse and I were going back to the armory that night to find out why the EOD team had visited Cumberland. If it confirmed what we expected, we were going to bypass Chief of Police Thompkins and go straight to Mayor Conklin.

I solved my wrapping problem by putting each of the gifts in a brown paper lunch bag. Then I rode to Christmas Eve service with Mom and Dad.

The church looked spectacular decorated from floor to ceiling in fresh evergreen boughs and illuminated by candles. Packed pews overflowed with believers and piles of coats waiting for the cold walk back to their cars. But as midnight neared and the church service came to a close, all hearts were warm.

I saw Pat Bandershot sitting alone glumly in the third pew. There was no sign of Dickerson.

We all sang the last few bars of "Silent Night" as the acolytes extinguished the candles. Then, holding the crucifer's cross, I led the processional out of the church. The bell tolled twelve times, and Christmas Day 1972 began.

"Merry Christmas, Reverend Cooper," I said as he passed me. He was massaging his right palm, tender from having shaken hands with every parishioner attending that night.

"I'm glad birthdays only come once a year. This was the big show. We'll be lucky to have twenty people at tomorrow's

Chapter Twenty-One - The Report

Christmas Day service. What do you want Santa to bring you, Shelby?"

"*Led Zeppelin IV.*"

Reverend Cooper's scowl dissuaded me from explaining more.

After changing, I met Jesse in the church's kitchen. My cover story with Mom and Dad was that Tim was picking me up for a party at his house. I found Jesse drinking from a gallon milk jug he'd procured from the church's refrigerator.

"Having a private communion, are you?"

Jesse wiped his mouth on his jean jacket sleeve. "Hey, I only get paid a buck fifty an hour here, so I need to take advantage of the fringe benefits. You got the keys to the armory?"

"Yup, where's your bus?"

"Right out back. Let's go."

It started snowing sometime during the service, leaving Jesse's VW bus covered in a light dusting of white, looking like a loaf of raisin bread ready for slicing.

When we got to the armory, we didn't bother being stealthy. Who was going to be there other than us? It was Christmas Eve. We turned on whatever lights we needed. Jesse went straight for the file cabinets in the breakroom next to Sergeant Inversol's office. It wasn't long before he found the October EOD report. Jesse sat at a table and started reading.

Looking around the room, I saw Colonel Bandershot's portable record player, the one we had used the first night we played Frisbee in the armory. Beside it was a stack of record albums. I assumed they were the march music Katie had said were left behind. What was odd was there was a large roll of duct tape sitting on top of the albums.

"Hey, Jesse, what's the duct tape for?"

Jesse looked up from the report annoyed and said, "When we drill in the gym, the squad leaders mark the floor with the duct tape to indicate where each group is to line up."

I leafed through the ten or so albums and laughed out loud when I was near the bottom of the stack. "It looks like someone's been sneaking in some unapproved music," I said while holding up an LP. "I don't remember any marches on *Abbey Road*."

"Will you shut up? I'm trying to read this thing," Jesse snapped, not looking up from the report.

Luckily, it was only ten pages long, and much of it was boilerplate material. Jesse found what he was looking for on page four.

Pushing back from the table, he took a breath through his nose and began to read aloud: "On the authority of the commander of Fort Meade, an explosive ordnance disposal team responded to a request for containment of a live-fire exercise site involving M67 fragmentation grenades at a location used by the Maryland National Guard of Cumberland on 15 September 1972. A unit of two EOD specialists was deployed on 1 October and

Chapter Twenty-One - The Report

completed their assignment in one day. Results: No unexploded or partially detonated M67s were found. The site was cleared of debris and is secure for reuse at this time."

I slammed my fist into my hand. "That clinches it. The EOD team was up here to look for unexploded grenades, and the date cited in the report jives with the entry date on Inversol's calendar, fifteen September. Dickerson must have pocketed one of the grenades."

"I don't know," said Jesse. "That wouldn't be easy to do. Inversol would have kept track of them."

"It doesn't matter; we've got him. I have to call Tim and have him warn Pat Bandershot. She's sleeping with a murderer." I picked up the wall phone and dialed Tim's number.

Tim's mom answered and made me promise to share Christmas wishes with my parents before putting Tim on the line.

I assured her I would as I heard Tim arguing, then rustling noises, then Tim's voice booming, "What's the word?"

"Don's dirty. Get over to Katie's house and warn her mom."

"Done," said Tim and hung up the phone.

I took the EOD report from Jesse. "Where's the copy machine?"

"In the maintenance room on the other side of the gym. Why?"

"I want to give a copy of the report to the mayor when I wake him up."

It took us about a half hour to make the copies because the machine was low on toner. Luckily, Jesse knew where the extra toner was, and while he topped off the machine, I went looking for an envelope to put the copy in. I found one in the acting commander's office as well as a jar of M&Ms. I grabbed a handful of the colorful candied vitamins and went back to help Jesse. With the copy neatly folded into the envelope and stashed in my back pocket, we confidently walked into the entry hall and were just about to open the front door when I said, "Wait, I want another dose of M&Ms."

I ducked into the commander's office and filled my hand again then heard a dull thud and the sound of something heavy hitting the floor.

"What the…" I said to myself then strained to hear anything else.

I heard nothing, so I uneasily tiptoed to the door and peeked into the entry hall.

"Get in here," Don Dickerson ordered as he stood over Jesse's body motioning to me with the .38-caliber pistol he had knocked Jesse out with. "Give me the report."

"What report?"

"Don't give me any of your shit. I overheard that doctor's boy telling Katie all about your little plan before church tonight. If you think I'm going to let you ruin my life, you're wrong. I want the investigation into Bandershot's death to stay closed, and there isn't anything I won't do to keep it that way. Give me that goddamn EOD report!" Dickerson yelled.

Chapter Twenty-One - The Report

"Okay, okay, it's in the bus. We stashed it under the passenger's seat and came back to throw Frisbees," I said as convincingly as I could. "Follow me, and I'll give it to you."

"And I'll want the seventh picture as well," Dickerson demanded.

His question threw me. "We only found six pictures. Who's in the seventh one?" I said as I slowly walked around Jesse—relieved to see he was still breathing. Dickerson made a hissing noise as I moved towards the door.

"If you don't have it, who does?" he seemed to say to no one as he tracked me with his gun.

As I opened the door, a cold spray of snow hit my face and made me turn away. Wiping my eyes clear, I looked at Dickerson. "I know you killed the colonel, but why did you kill Sergeant Inversol?"

Dickerson jammed the barrel of the revolver into my back. "I didn't kill him. I wanted him dead, but he killed himself before I could get around to it. Keep moving. You're not going to talk your way out of this."

We were almost to the VW, and the M&Ms were beginning to melt in my hand. If I was going to make a move, I had to make it fast, or this was my last snowstorm.

"HONK! HONK! HONK! Bellowed the unmistakable sound of a Cadillac Eldorado's horn.

We both looked up to see headlights cresting the hill only fifty yards away as Pat Bandershot's land yacht jumped the curb and headed straight for us over the lawn of the armory.

I threw my handful of M&Ms in Dickerson's face, and he jerked as they hit him. His gun went off, and a bullet whistled past my ear.

I ran for the woods.

This only bought me a couple of seconds as Dickerson recovered and ran after me screaming, "Stop, or I'll shoot. STOP!"

The gun went off again just as I passed into the darkness of the pathway through the trees to the cliffs. I was running as fast as I could, but the light snow made the ground slippery—I bounced off a limb or two as I went.

The trees were bare, and the snow reflected the moonshine, making it easier to see than I expected, but what I saw scared me to death. I was running with all my might straight at an exposed cliff with nowhere to hide and nowhere to go but down.

I glanced back over my shoulder just as Dickerson fired another round that struck a tree to my right. I felt shards of wood hit my arm as I pushed hard for my last ounce of speed. I could see the opening ahead and the ledge reflecting the moonlight.

"What are you going to do when you get there—fly?" I asked myself.

Chapter Twenty-One - The Report

An image flashed into my mind from that day four months earlier when Tim and I hid the beer in the cave. There was Tim, with a beer in his hand, hanging on the rope and spinning like a circling bird.

"The rope!" My subconscious screamed. I strained my eyes to see if I could discern the inch-thick strand dangling somewhere in the dark near the edge of the cliff, but the snow hitting my face made it difficult.

"Stop!" Dickerson yelled again just as I broke free of the woods.

There it was, the rope. Right where Tim had left it. I lunged for it, hoping I could swing over to the other ledge about ten yards to the right.

My right hand got a good grip, but my left one slipped on the wet hemp as I sailed off the ledge into the snowy night air.

The view was spectacular. I could see the Potomac River far below me and the moon reflecting off its cold waters, and I wondered if this was my last view on earth. I was barely hanging on, and the other ledge was coming on fast, but my momentum was not quite enough to reach it.

My heart sank as I reached the apex of my flight and rotated to start my return to Dickerson.

He had stopped at the edge of the cliff and was standing like a cop at a firing range holding his pistol with both hands and aiming at me.

Just as I was close enough to see the little colored spots on Dickerson's face left by my melting M&Ms, I heard a booming voice yell, "No, you don't, you piece of shit," as Pat Bandershot reared back like Trigger and kicked Don Dickerson square in the back with her patent leather Gucci pumps.

Don's gun went off for the last time as he launched—stomach first—off the cliff and down to the rhododendrons.

My rope swing was over and the toe of my shoe touched the ledge.

"Come here, you idiot," Pat Bandershot said as she grabbed my belt and pulled me to safety. "Thanks for the warning."

"You're welcome," I gasped as Tim and Katie bounded out of the woods. We all looked over the cliff at Don, still alive but impaled on the leafless branches below.

Chapter Twenty-Two
All is Calm

Jesse had a mild concussion and spent the night in the hospital under observation, but he was okay. Don Dickerson was not. He had a broken leg and needed ninety-seven stitches for twenty-one wounds. After being arrested for murder, he quickly cut a plea deal to avoid life in prison.

He confessed to killing Colonel Bandershot, and we all attended his arraignment along with Pat.

After the bailiff called the court to order and the judge entered, Don was asked to describe his murder plot.

"Your honor, I was in love and not thinking straight. This is not an excuse, just the reality of why I did what I did. I tried to convince Mrs. Bandershot to run away with me, but she wouldn't leave her husband before her daughter finished college. In my clouded mind, I couldn't wait that long, so the colonel had to go."

Pat Bandershot stirred in her chair. "I never intended to leave with that loser."

The judge banged his gavel, and the bailiff said, "Order in the court."

Head slumped, Dickerson continued, "I used Sergeant Inversol as a tool to accomplish my plan. I befriended him, bought him drinks, and lent him money. I leveraged his drug addiction, convincing him to give me access to the armory's grenades. I want you to know the sergeant was hesitant at first, but his weaknesses worked in my favor."

"Poor Jack," Katie whispered to her mother.

Pat Bandershot squeezed Katie's hand. "I understand now."

"He arranged for us to meet at the armory's firing range. He brought three grenades and let me throw them. I threw the first two, and they exploded. I only pretended to pull the arming pin on the last one before throwing it, and Sergeant Inversol thought it was a dud. I went back to the range later and retrieved the unexploded grenade. I used it to booby trap the tank and kill Colonel Bandershot, knowing Sergeant Inversol would be the Army's number one suspect."

I nudged Tim. "Never mix morphine with grenades."

"Shush," Tim hissed.

Dickerson went on to tell how he learned of the EOD team and its report from Major Bennington. Bennington had found it on Inversol's desk along with his suicide note, but he deemed it unimportant, figuring Inversol was just at The Pit practicing for the murder.

Don hoped the report would remain locked in the armory's file cabinet. It didn't occur to him that Inversol might have made a calendar entry with his name on it or that four kids would tie the two things together.

"Mr. Dickerson, how did you gain access to the tank?" the judge asked.

Chapter Twenty-Two - All is Calm

"Late on the night before the ceremony, I visited Sergeant Inversol at the armory. He was alone, and I helped him cover the tank with a tarp. He was heavily intoxicated and barely functioning, so it wasn't hard for me to slip into the tank and hang the grenade from the hatch opening by a string connected to the arming pin."

I whispered to Tim, "That must be who Jesse saw on the tank that night."

Tim nodded.

The arraignment ended with the judge delaying sentencing till after Dickerson was healthy enough to go to jail. He was expected to get fifteen years without the possibility of parole.

We drove home with Mrs. Bandershot behind the wheel of her Eldorado. "I want you children to know I was not involved in this crime in any way."

We were all silent as it was clear she didn't require confirmation.

Katie leaned forward from the back seat. "Don probably thought he was in the clear when Jack killed himself, bringing the investigation to a close quickly."

Tim pulled her back and hugged her. "Right. Don's perfect plan didn't start to unravel until he overheard me telling you we knew about the report. That was when he took the actions that led to his downfall, both figuratively and literally."

I turned to Mrs. Bandershot and touched her shoulder. "Thank heaven, you decided to drive to the armory and confront Don."

"Men!" Pat Bandershot said with exasperation. "I've got to get away from this place and clear my head."

And she did. The day after the trial Mrs. Bandershot flew to Miami Beach. She expected the sordid details of the key club to be in the paper any day, and she didn't want to be around when they were. Katie refused to go with her, and her Mom didn't argue. Katie had grown up a lot in the past few days.

Surprisingly, the anticipated scandal didn't materialize. Life in Cumberland tumbled forward, and the words key club never appeared in newsprint.

A few days later, after hearing my tape recording, the police raided Doctor Huntler's dental office, and they arrested him on drug charges. He had thirty times the permitted amount of morphine in his supply cabinet. At his arraignment, he threw himself on the mercy of the court and confessed to everything, including sewing up Sergeant Inversol's gunshot wound with dental floss.

The Army JAG corps acknowledged their error, but before they reassessed the Bandershot murder case, they promoted Major Stan Bennington to lieutenant colonel and assigned him to the Nixon White House.

Chief of Police Thompkins was quietly demoted and assigned patrol duty in South Cumberland. No official explanation was given.

Chapter Twenty-Two - All is Calm

With Sergeant Jack Inversol's name cleared, on December twenty-eighth, the Maryland National Guard conducted a formal funeral with full military honors at his grave site. Katie, Tim, Jesse, and I attended.

I explained everything to Mom and Dad and endured an hour of questions before they revoked my driving privileges for a month. Things swung back to normal, and I enjoyed the rest of my holiday vacation. I was glad the craziness of the last few months was over.

I was wrong.

Chapter Twenty-Three
Tie Clip

Tim didn't see Katie for two days. She retreated into her big empty house and lost herself in memories of her father and Jack. When Katie called Tim on December thirtieth, she said she'd cried enough and wanted to have a New Year's Eve party. Tim was glad she had resurfaced and said he'd have me get the beer.

Jesse was invited, too, and since he had finally gotten a new battery for his bus and as I was suspended from the Barracuda, I volunteered him to drive. It was easy to motivate him to come since Katie promised to ask some other girls to the party so we wouldn't be lonely.

It was a rainy nine o'clock on New Year's Eve morning when Jesse picked me up to do our duty. He wanted to buy the beer before he had to start work at the church at eleven.

I climbed into the passenger seat of his VW. "How about we go out to Pop Snyder's place in West Virginia? We can get all the beer we need plus any snacks we want."

Jesse jammed the shifter into first, and the bus jumped forward like a startled cat. "I'm not driving out Route 28 in this shitty wet weather. My tires are bald, and that road is crooked enough to run for governor."

I handed Jesse three dollars to cover part of the cost. "But you have to be twenty-one to buy beer in Maryland."

Chapter Twenty-Three - Tie Clip

"Yeah, I know, but even though my twenty-first birthday is still six months away, I never get carded. I guess it's just my good looks and winning personality," Jesse joked.

"Right, I'm sure it has nothing to do with you being six-foot-four and weighing two fifty," I said. "Okay, where do you want to get the beer?"

"Parkview Liquors is closest, and they have snacks too." Jesse steered the beige bus down the street.

Jesse parked, and being only seventeen, I let him go in to do the buying. As he disappeared around the corner, I realized I forgot to tell him to buy me some beef jerky, my favorite *hors d'oeuvre* with beer. I climbed out of the bus and followed him.

The front of Parkview Liquors was a cacophony of neon lights swirling and blinking their siren song to the thirsty masses. As I entered the glass door covered in booze advertisements, I saw Jesse near the back stacking six-packs of beer into a cardboard box. I looked around for the beef jerky, and finding it, I selected four of my favorites and got into the checkout line.

I didn't know the clerk operating the cash register, but he looked familiar. What he didn't look like was the rest of the Parkview Liquors employees. Parkview men were clean-cut good ol' boys who loved Dick Nixon, country music, and football. The clerk's hair was long, and he was wearing a white oxford shirt with a wide paisley tie—way too preppy for Cumberland.

Jesse finished paying, and it was my turn. I took a step forward and placed my culinary treats on the counter. That's when I saw the clerk's tie clip. Stunned, it was as if someone sent a thousand volts through my body. There at the center of his tie clip between the words University and Michigan was a nickel-sized enamel embossed disk with two letters on it: Delta Phi.

"Is this all?" the clerk asked me. "Just the beef jerky?"

I looked up from his tie clip, but as I did, I saw his name tag, and I felt the electricity again as my stomach flipped and my knees weakened. In big white letters on his black plastic name tag were two more letters: ED.

"Hey, kid. Are you going to buy those or not?" the man behind me said as he nudged me with his case of beer.

"Ahh, sure. This is all I want. How much?" I finally forced out of my throat.

Ed from Delta Phi punched open the cash register. "Eighty-nine cents will do it. Do you need a bag?"

"No, thanks." I slipped a dollar from my pocket, placed it on the counter, and turned for the door.

"Don't you want your change?" Ed called to me.

I kept walking. Back at the bus, I jumped in and said, "Let's get out of here."

"Hold your water, boy, I want to put some music on," Jesse said as he started the bus and pushed the eight-track tape he

Chapter Twenty-Three - Tie Clip

had in his hand into the player. The folk rock sounds of James Taylor singing "You've Got a Friend" filled the air.

As Jesse pulled out of the parking lot, I tried to process what I'd seen in Parkview and fit it in with all that had happened in the past few weeks. Then it hit me. Petrified, I looked down at the eight-track then at Jesse.

"James Taylor," I said.

Jesse's eyes darted in my direction. "Yeah, black men are allowed to listen to folk rock, too, you know."

"No, he's James Taylor," I said louder. "Pull over. I need to tell you something."

"Are you nuts?"

"Just pull over—now!"

Jesse steered the bus into a parking space. "Okay, what's so damned important?"

"That long-haired guy at Parkview. He looks like James Taylor, and he had on a Delta Phi fraternity tie clip."

"Yeah, so what? I'm thinking of joining a frat out at the college myself," Jesse said.

"No, don't you remember? Delta Phi were the two Greek letters at the bottom of Sergeant Inversol's suicide note, and Tim saw Inversol arguing with a James Taylor look-alike at Colonel Bandershot's funeral."

Jesse shifted in his seat. "Wait a minute. Didn't you tell me Katie said Don was a frat guy, and we already know he's a killer? Maybe he killed Inversol. He had a good reason; Inversol knew about him and the grenades."

I shook Jesse's arm. "Don told me he didn't kill Inversol and he didn't expect me to be around long enough to tell anyone, so, I believe him. Listen, there's more. The Parkview guy's name is Ed. Jesse, think about it. Ed was the name Inversol wrote on the back of one of the nude photos next to the Parkview Liquors phone number. This guy is dirty."

Jesse pursed his lips and furrowed his brow. "That might be something."

"We have to find out about this guy Ed," I said.

"But how?" asked Jesse. "Go back and ask if he's arranged any drug overdoses lately?"

"Let me think." I didn't want to go to the police or the mayor, at least not yet. "Take me to Peskin's."

Jesse looked at me and smiled. "Why, do you need new shoes?"

"No, my mom works there, and she knows everyone in this town. Maybe she can help."

Jesse pulled into traffic. "Okay, I'll play along, but I've only got forty-five minutes before I'm due at work."

We found Mom taking the skirt off a mannequin in one of the three floor-to-ceiling display windows on the ground floor of Peskin's. I was about to knock on the thick glass between mom and us when Mort Peskin came out of the store with a pair of ladies' shoes in his hand.

Chapter Twenty-Three - Tie Clip

"Here you go, Stel," Mort said to Mom as he leaned in through the display case's glass door.

"No, Mort, I need the peach-colored ones, not red," Mom said as she pulled a different skirt onto the mannequin's frame.

"Right, Stel." Mort eyed Jesse from head to toe. "Wow! Did you play tackle or guard in school, son?"

"Trombone, Mr. Peskin. I was in the Allegany band."

Mort turned to me. "That father of yours can talk an elephant into a tutu. If he ever quits teaching, tell him he'd make a great shoe salesman."

"Hey, Mr. Peskin, maybe you can help us. If you had to find out about a person's background, but you didn't want them to know you were doing it, who would you talk to," I asked, thinking Mort would know more than Mom about things like this.

Mr. Peskin's head tilted back a bit as he squinted his eyes. "What are you guys up to, checking out some hot new dame in town?"

"You can't say dame anymore, Mort!" Mom yelled through the glass.

"Sorry, Stel." Mr. Peskin shook his head and smirked. "But what's the deal, boys?"

I was about to spill the real story when Jesse said, "A new guy is working at Parkview Liquors who looks a lot like someone I was in basic with at Fort Benning, but I'm not sure. The guy

I knew went AWOL halfway through the course. I don't want to get him in any trouble, so I thought we could do a little background check first. All I need is his last name and hometown to be sure."

Mr. Peskin was quiet for a minute then looked at Mom. She had stepped out of the glass box and into her shoes. She always worked barefoot in the display windows. I had a feeling she was about to nix the whole thing, so I piped up. "Like Jesse says, he doesn't want to get this guy in trouble. If Jesse's right, we'll just let him know we know, and maybe he'll move on."

"Vietnam is history, Mr. Peskin," Jesse added. "Henry Kissinger recently announced we're near a peace deal, so I'm not looking to get anyone arrested for draft dodging. I'd rather see him avoid it, but two other Cumberland guys were at basic with us, and they may feel differently."

Mr. Peskin's head dropped back to its normal position, and he made a sucking sound with his teeth before saying, "Frankie Adams. Let's walk down to Frankie Adams's office at the *Cumberland Times*. If he can't help you, no one can."

Jesse punched me softly on the arm. "I guess I'm going to miss work."

Chapter Twenty-Four
Smile

Mr. Peskin grabbed two umbrellas from inside the store and led us to the *Cumberland Times* office building, only three blocks down the street. After going up a flight of stairs, we found ourselves in an open bay office crowded with four desks, each staffed by a reporter. One was shining his shoes, two where reading newspapers, and the fourth was sound asleep. The place smelled of ashtrays, hot metal, and ink.

"Slow news day," Mr. Peskin commented.

We weaved our way through the maze of men and chairs then stopped at a glassed-in office that reminded me of Mom's display window, only dirtier. Mr. Peskin knocked, and an older man stood from his desk and came to the door. To say he stood wasn't accurate because he was suffering from a debilitating back problem that forced him into a permanent crescent-like stance. To look us in the face, he had to lift his head like we would to see something on the ceiling.

"What do you need, Mort?" Franklin T. Adams, the morning desk editor, said as he opened the door.

Mr. Peskin shook the man's hand. "Frankie, you typesetting son of a bitch, if you keep curling over, you're going to look like a zero."

"Better to look like a zero than to be one like you," Frankie said. "Come on in, you hair-hat-wearing mashugana."

Mr. Peskin grinned and pretended to adjust the jet-black toupee that covered his prematurely bald head.

The editor returned to his chair and was greatly relieved when he could sit back down. Mr. Peskin leaned on his desk. "I need to tap that infinite well of knowledge of yours, Frankie. There's a new guy at Parkview Liquors that may be hiding something about his past, and I want to know if it's serious enough to involve the police."

Frankie pointed to a well-worn piece of furniture covered in newsprint. "Put those papers on the floor, boys, and sit on the couch. Why do you care about this, Mort?"

"I spend a lot of money at Parkview and don't want it going out of business because some loser robs it. Boys, tell him what you know."

Jesse told the story he shared with Mr. Peskin, and after a few seconds of thought, Mr. Adams said, "That's not much to go on. All you've got is his first name is Ed, he works at Parkview, and he might be a draft dodger?"

"Well, there is one more thing," I said. "He was a member of the Delta Phi fraternity at the University of Michigan. He's wearing one of their tie clips."

Mr. Adams was quiet for a few more seconds. "Okay, that's something. If I had a photo of him, I could wire it to a buddy of mine at the *Ann Arbor Michigan News*. He might be able to help."

Mr. Peskin looked at Jesse and me as if to ask if that was enough, but before we could answer, Mr. Adams interrupted.

Chapter Twenty-Four - Smile

"Listen, we're dying for news today. Nothing ever happens on New Year's Eve, and who knows, if this Ed turns out to be a bad guy, it might make a good story. How about I send One-Shot Charlie with you up to Parkview so we can get a picture of this guy? We run ads for them twice weekly so we can say you're there for that reason."

"Great," Jesse said. "When can we do that?"

Mr. Adams started to get up, grimaced, and changed his mind. "Would now be too soon? One-Shot's next assignment isn't until late afternoon when the mayor crowns the New Year's queen."

Mr. Peskin stood. "Perfect, I've got to get to the dry cleaner's and pick up my tux for the New Year's party tonight, or my wife will kill me. You're on your own, boys."

Mr. Adams nodded. "Right, Mort, I'll see you there, but I'm not dancing with you."

With his right arm out straight and his left one curled, Mr. Peskin pretended to waltz out of the office.

Fifteen minutes later, Jesse and I found ourselves in a *Cumberland Times* paneled truck driven by One-Shot Charlie. We were relegated to the back of the truck along with several bundles of newspapers because the passenger seat was reserved for Charlie's beloved Graflex Speed Graphic press camera.

Charles Sturbridge was ungracefully sliding into his sixties and hadn't bought a new suit since the Truman administration. He looked a lot like Cliff Arquette's Charley Weaver character from *Hollywood Squares* and got the nickname One-Shot because of his diligence in never wasting film. He'd show up at his assignment, position himself correctly, and only when the time was right, snap the one photo he needed for the story.

"What's this guy look like?" One-Shot asked as he illegally parked the truck in front of Parkview Liquors.

"James Taylor," I answered.

Charlie twisted around to look at me. "Who in the hell is James Taylor?"

Jesse cut in. "You just ask me, and I'll let you know if it's him or not."

Our photographer carefully lifted the toaster-sized camera from the seat next to him. "Okay, come with me and point him out."

It was quiet in Parkview, and Ed was nowhere in sight. The only other person was behind the counter working a crossword puzzle.

One-Shot walked up to the guy. "Mr. Adams from the *Times* told me to stop by and get some photos for next week's ad on the big New Year's sale."

"Okay, do you need me to do anything?" asked the clerk.

"Nope, let me just check the lighting in here." Charlie looked at Jesse for confirmation as to whether or not this guy was Ed.

Jesse shook his head. "Is Ed working today?"

"Yeah, he's in the back doing inventory," the clerk said.

Chapter Twenty-Four - Smile

One-Shot pointed at his camera. "Why don't you ask him to come in and I'll get a shot of the two of you behind the counter doing God's work?"

Moving to a curtained doorway near the back of the store the clerk yelled, "Hey, Ed! Get in here for a minute!"

We heard some rustling, then footsteps, and Charlie lifted his camera. As Ed pushed through the curtain and looked up to see what was going on, Charlie said, "Smile" and took a picture. The flash was blinding and left a black spot at the center of everyone's eyesight.

Charlie started fiddling with the camera as Ed stopped dead in his tracks and looked at each of us with anger. Then he spun around and returned to the back room.

The clerk laughed. "I guess he's shy."

"No problem, I'll take one out front and be going. Thanks," said One-Shot, and we all hurried out of the store.

While driving back to the newspaper, Charlie told us he'd get the photo developed and give it to the editor in a couple of hours. He dropped us off at Jesse's bus.

We drove through downtown's urban-renewal-clad storefronts, once a glory of architectural design. "What time are we to be at Katie's for the party?" Jesse asked.

"Any time after nine."

"Right. That gives us some time to unwind." Jesse turned onto a residential street that ended at a pockmarked field.

Winter's early darkness was closing down the day, and the rain had let up, but the sky promised more.

Jesse turned off the car and reached behind his seat and pulled a beer from one of the six-packs. "Here, man, it's good to go. I got them out of the refrigerator."

"Thanks, aren't you going to have one?"

"No, I need some weed."

"I thought you were taking a break from that?"

"Break's over. I thought we were finished with this murder case, but now we're back in the middle of it. All this interaction with the police makes me nervous, and now we have the newspaper involved."

I sipped on my beer as Jesse lit up the joint he retrieved from the glove box. "You see those bumps in the field?" Jesse said as he inhaled most of the inch-long reefer in one drag.

"Yeah, what causes that?"

"That's Potter's Field, and those dents in the ground are all that's left of a lot of my people." Jesse lit up another joint.

I looked out the side window. "Potter's Field?"

"It's an indigent graveyard where the city disposes of bodies," Jesse said.

I looked again, and this time, I realized the indentations in the ground were regularly spaced and about the size of a grave.

Chapter Twenty-Four - Smile

"If you're black and die without any money or end up dead after a fight with the police, that's where they put you," Jesse pointed at the field. "My Uncle Buck is out there somewhere. We're not sure where because the city didn't keep good records, but he's one of those ruts in the weeds."

"What happened?" I asked.

"I don't know the whole story, but he was the black sheep of the family, always drunk and always in jail. He got drafted when the war started, but his drinking didn't stop, and he deserted soon afterward. The family disowned him and figured he was gone for good until he came back to Cumberland in '49. His brain was pickled, and he lived on the streets. We'd call him homeless today, but back then, he was a bum. The cops found him dead in a B&O boxcar in South Cumberland and buried him out there not knowing who he was. It was a year before Dad found out, and too late to identify Buck's grave, so he left him there."

"Happy story," I said.

Jesse lifted his joint and nodded. "Yeah, Happy New Year, Uncle Buck. So, what would you like to do between now and the party?

"I'll tell you what I want to do. I want to go back to Parkview Liquors and talk to Ed. Did you see the way he looked at us? That guy is hiding something."

Jesse coughed, and smoke shot out of his nose. "Are you kidding? If you are right and he is involved in Inversol's death, he may finish what Don Dickerson started and push you off a cliff. Here's an alternative; I'm hungry. Let's get something to eat."

"I hear you, but I'm worried Ed's going to turn rabbit and run, and then we'll never know anything. Listen, let's go to my place for a sandwich. There's still tons of turkey leftover from Christmas dinner."

"Cool," said Jesse as he tossed his dead doobie out the window and started the bus.

We fixed sandwiches and watched the *CBS Evening News* with Walter Cronkite on the twelve-inch black-and-white TV in my kitchen. The big story of the day was the stock market closing at an all-time high of one thousand twenty.

Mom and Dad said goodbye as they passed through the kitchen and left for the same party Mort Peskin would be going to. The marijuana mellowed Jesse's mood, and the two turkey sandwiches scratched his hunger itch, so I was able to convince him to go back to Parkview. I told him we'd avoid Ed and only talk to other employees. Maybe they could shed some light on Ed's background.

The telephone rang as I pulled the back door closed. I looked at Jesse. "You better answer; it might be important."

I opened the door and walked to the phone. "Hello."

"Shelby, this is Mr. Adams down at the *Cumberland Times*. Is your mom or dad there?"

"No, sir, just Jesse and me. Did you get the photo from One-Shot?"

Chapter Twenty-Four - Smile

"Yes, I did, and I don't have to wire it to Michigan. The guy in the photo may be a member of the Weathermen Underground, that radical anti-war group that bombed the Pentagon last May. The FBI sends us all their Most Wanted lists, and one from six months ago has a guy on it named Edward Stickley that looks a lot like your Ed, only with shorter hair. It's a blurry candid photo, not one of their formal mug shots, but it could be him. I'm going to notify the police, and I want you to stay away from this guy. He's dangerous."

I assured Mr. Adams we would do as he said, then hung up the phone and went out to Jesse's bus.

"Who was that?" Jesse asked.

"No one. It was a wrong number."

Chapter Twenty-Five
Déjà vu

We parked in shadows behind Parkview and walked around to the front door. There were a few last-minute shoppers picking up supplies for New Year's parties but no Ed.

Jesse tapped a worker restocking a shelf with vodka and asked, "Is Ed here?"

"Nope, he left just a couple of minutes ago. Can I help you find something?"

"No thanks. Is there a manager on duty?"

"Yeah, Mr. Robinette's in the back."

"Thanks," Jesse said and went looking for the manager.

I walked around hoping to talk to other coworkers of Ed's, but they were all busy with customers, so I marveled at the sheer number of choices we Americans had when it came to booze. I counted no fewer than twenty-three varieties of bourbon, and I was busy counting the gin choices when Jesse tapped my shoulder. "Time to go. I need another smoke."

Seeing Jesse, I realized I had to tell him about the call from Mr. Adams, so I finished counting the gin brands—there were eighteen—and followed him, but he got to the car before I did. The rain had started again, and it was so dark I could only see the outline of the VW bus, but I heard Jesse's door slam as I made my way around to the passenger's side.

Chapter Twenty-Five - Déjà vu

I was reaching for the door handle when an arm wrapped around my neck and choked off my windpipe. "Let's make this as simple as possible," said the arm's voice. "I have a gun pointed at your head, and if you don't do exactly as I say; well, just do as I say."

I felt the barrel of the gun against my right temple as he released his grip enough for me to breathe. "Okay," I gasped.

"I want you to open the door slowly," said the man as he tightened his grip again, this time partially lifting me off the ground. "But don't do anything stupid."

I nodded and opened the bus door.

Jesse was in the process of lighting up a reefer. When he saw Ed and his gun behind my frightened face, he dropped the joint into his lap. Hopping and brushing his pants with his hand to avoid being burned, he said, "Let him go. We'll do what you want, but let him go."

Ed released his arm from my neck but kept the gun against my temple. "Open up the side door for me," he said to Jesse, and Jesse slid out of his seat and undid the bungee cord from the side door handle.

As the bus door opened, Ed said to me, "Get in the passenger seat." He looked at Jesse. "You get behind the wheel."

We did as he ordered and watched as he got in and closed the side door. Our damp kidnapper sat in the center of the rear bench seat with his gun pointed at us. His face was manic intensity changing James Taylor into Norman Bates.

"Gentlemen, how nice of you to return. Did you think I didn't notice your interest in me today?"

"What are you talking about?" Jesse asked.

"Don't play dumb with me; you're not smart enough." Ed tapped his gun to the roof of the bus as if to remind us that he had it. "What do you know?"

"I know from your manager that you've only been in town for four months and don't fit in very well with the rest of the Parkview Liquors staff," Jesse said.

I interrupted him. "And your name is Edward Stickley, you're a member of the Weathermen Underground, and you were with them when they bombed the Pentagon earlier this year."

Jesse looked at me like I was a unicorn.

"Sorry, Jesse. That call I got wasn't a wrong number, it was Mr. Adams from the newspaper. He recognized this guy from an FBI's Most Wanted list." I kept my eyes on our captor. "Stickley, you better let us go and get out of here fast. Mr. Adams called the police, and they are most likely on their way here right now."

With the flick of his wrist, Stickley slammed his gun against my cheek. It sounded like a fly swatter ending a buzz, but it felt like a mule's kick. "Shut up, boy. I give zero fucks for the Cumberland police. I've got a job to finish and a get-out-of-jail-free card anyway."

Stickley pulled what looked like a large folded photo from his raincoat pocket. "If the police give me any trouble, all I have

Chapter Twenty-Five - Déjà vu

to do is show them this. Now get this bus started and drive to the Blue Bridge. It's time for you to visit West Virginia."

The rain intensified as we crossed the Potomac River, and the old bus's headlights struggled to light the road ahead, brightening as Jesse accelerated and dimming as he braked.

"Where are we going?" Jesse asked.

"Just stay on Route 28; it's not far now," Stickley said.

I looked at Stickley. "This job of yours, it involved Sergeant Inversol, didn't it?"

"He was accommodating, but only up to a point."

"And then you killed him," Jesse said.

Stickley snickered. "Well, he was already halfway there that night. I just helped him over the finish line. He'd be in Costa Rica now enjoying his money if he'd done as we planned, but no, he had an attack of moral conscience."

The road opened up as we left the confines of the small town across the river from Cumberland, and before us were the twisting curves of West Virginia Route 28. As we snaked our way south, to our left and thirty feet down a steep embankment was the Potomac River. On the right, a wall of shale rose sharply, leaving no room for navigation error.

"Did you force him to write the suicide note?" Jesse asked.

"That wasn't a suicide note; it was a confession. He was planning on signing it and hand-delivering it to the JAG major the next day, and he would have if I hadn't stopped him halfway."

"What do you mean halfway?" I asked.

Stickley snickered smugly. "I think Jack's next paragraph would have told of our deal and how he wasn't going through with it. I persuaded him he had written enough and that it was time to sign. I suggested Jack toast his note's completions with a little bourbon. I forgot to tell him I'd tripled the morphine dosage. He was eager for a hit and chugged it right down. It wasn't long before he was sleeping like a baby. Well, maybe more like a doornail. It was the investigators who misread his scribbles as a suicide note."

"What was the deal?" Jesse asked.

"That's all. You don't need to know anything more," Stickley said. "Speed up. The limit is forty-five on this road, and you're only going thirty. I've got a lot I have to do tonight after I take care of you guys."

My cheek was beginning to swell, and it hurt when I said, "Where are you taking us?"

"Right where you belong, with the rest of the Cumberland garbage," Stickley said as he tapped his gun on the right-side window directing our attention. A sign reading City Dump Two Miles whizzed past us.

"Hey, put on some music. Let's liven this ride up," Stickley ordered.

Jesse looked at me and nodded towards the floor. I bent down and grabbed the first eight-track I found. My hands were shaking so much I had trouble pushing it into the

Chapter Twenty-Five - Déjà vu

machine. Jimi Hendrix sang, "There must be some kinda way out of here, said the joker to the thief."

The rain got heavier and streaked along the sides of the bus, looking like walls of blue water rushing past us. I'm sure I looked scared, but when I glanced over at Jesse, his face was awake with astonishment, as if he saw something magical. He was staring straight ahead—eyes fixed—and his mouth was slack-jawed as he sucked in a breath quickly.

I looked through the blurry windshield, hoping to see what had Jesse's attention, but I saw nothing except a bright yellow diamond-shaped warning sign depicting a swerving car sliding in a double-S pattern.

"Slippery when wet," Jesse said in almost a whisper.

"What'd he say?" Stickley asked.

"Slippery when wet," Jesse said louder. Then he yelled at the top of his lungs, "Sally!" and slammed on the brakes and turned the steering wheel sharply to the right.

The VW bus's bald tires gave way, and the back end swung out like a screen door. We tilted up onto the two left wheels, and I grabbed the armrest to stop from falling off my seat. Stickley had nothing to grab and was tossed like a rag doll against the left side of the bus.

Jesse reversed his turn and spun the steering wheel as far to the left as he could. The bus slammed down on all four wheels again and skidded towards the steep shale mountainside.

Stickley's vector changed, but his velocity stayed the same, and he flew across the cabin towards the bus's side doors.

Slippery When Wet

Unsecured by the bungee cord, they gave way as he hit, and he sailed out into the rainy void tightly gripping his gun. He no longer had a smug look on his face.

Something flew in front of me caught in the whirlwind—it was Stickley's folded photo. He must have dropped it when he slammed against the bus wall.

I grabbed for the picture as the bus tilted up on its two right wheels, and I was sure we were going all the way over this time, but the mountain stopped our roll. There was the sound of ten thousand garbage disposals, each devouring a teaspoon as the sharp shale of the mountainside snapped the open doors off and scraped every inch of paint from the side of the bus. The bus bounced down on all fours again, and Jesse regained control just as I trapped the eight-by-ten against the side window. We swerved back onto the road and accelerated into the soggy night as Jimi Hendrix finished his song.

"It was her!" Jesse yelled to be heard over the wind whipping through the opening in the side of the bus. "It was Grandma Sally telling me what to do."

"You mean the sign?" I asked.

"That was no sign. It was Sally. She saved us."

I looked back at the sign, now fading into the distance.

"Thank you, Sally."

Chapter Twenty-Six
The Metric System

It was noisy and cold, but the bus was drivable, and Jesse steered us to Katie's house.

I turned on the overhead dome light and looked at Stickley's get-out-of-jail-free photo.

It was exactly like the other ones from Sergeant Inversol's collection. It showed Pat Bandershot with a man, and they were engaged in adult activities, but they were not having sex. This photo had a man dressed in a skintight leather bodysuit with a rubber ball stuck in his mouth. He was down on all fours like a dog with Pat standing over him in a negligee and Nazi SS officer's hat. She was pulling on a choke-chain around his neck as her right high heel pushed forcefully into the center of his back. She was also paddling his rear end with a riding crop.

I held up the photo for Jesse to see. "I guess this is number seven; do you recognize the bow-wow? It's Mayor Conklin."

Jesse shook his head. "White folk."

Arriving at Katie's, we were almost to the front door when we were startled by the Eldorado's horn as it pulled in behind us.

"What in the world happened to the VW? It looks like it lost a fight with a carwash," Tim said as he swung the Cadillac's half-ton door shut.

"It wasn't a carwash; it was Sergeant Inversol's killer," Jesse said as he marveled at the mangled mess that once was his beloved bus.

"Who killed Jack?" Katie asked.

"Let's get in out of the rain, and we'll tell you all about it. You don't have to worry about him anymore. We sort of ejected him from the picture."

Jesse pulled on my sleeve. "We need to call the police and tell them Stickley's part of a mountain on Route 28."

"Okay, I guess so, but I'm not doing it."

Katie directed us into her dad's den, and I asked her to make an anonymous call to the police and tell them where they could find a guy named Ed Stickley and then call her friends and cancel the party.

"Why me?" Katie asked.

"A girl's voice will keep them off our trail."

Katie shook her head and left. After I was sure she was gone, I showed Tim the seventh picture.

"Jesus, that's the mayor getting spanked."

I laughed. "Yes, and he seems to be enjoying it."

"Put it away before Katie sees it," Tim said.

"No problem."

The colonel's room was paneled in stained wood and surrounded in bookcases except for one wall. It was

Chapter Twenty-Six - The Metric System

dedicated to glorifying himself. Photos of Mike Bandershot in different uniforms at various times in his career—as well as diplomas and certificates—plastered the wall.

There was a photo of the colonel with his men waiting to load the ship that would deliver them to Normandy, and one of him being awarded a medal somewhere, and many others. Interspersed with the pictures were the weapons of war the colonel's profession required. There was a sidearm like the one Sergeant Inversol pointed at us at the armory, a rifle, two swords, and a bayonet.

On the table in front of the wall were more military toys including a green ammunition box, several clips containing multiple bullets, and an unfortunately now ironic M67 grenade. This one was painted blue to indicate it was inert, unlike the one the colonel encountered in the tank.

Katie returned. "Okay, the cops are happy and on their way to scrape Stickley off the road. Oh, and the party is officially canceled."

"Thanks," I said and spent the next few minutes telling Katie and Tim all about what had happened to Jesse and me. I didn't share the Sally apparition part of the story but made it clear we knew who the Delta Phi fraternity boy was and his involvement in Jack Inversol's death.

There were a few seconds of silence until Katie asked, "So, this guy Stickley was part of the Weathermen Underground, and he forced Jack to overdose after signing the note?"

"Yes. But he didn't force Jack to drink; he spiked his bottle with a lethal dose. They were working some deal, but Jack changed his mind, and Stickley wasn't happy."

Tim sighed. "Wow, I thought we had the big news of the night. But we didn't dump a murderer out of our car going sideways on Route 28."

I put a plastic baggy of ice Katie had brought me on my now bluish cheek. "What big news do you have?"

Tim, ever the doctor's son, lifted up the bag of ice from my face and looked at my wound. "Katie wanted to know how we figured out the connection between the EOD report and Don, so I told her all about that and the other clues we discovered in Jack's office stuff. Oh, and that's going to leave a mark." Tim let the ice bag fall gently back onto my cheek.

Katie took over and said, "The first part of our news is I think I know what the letters of the math problem stand for on the back of the Parkview Liquors receipt—you know, the M, C, and K."

She paused waiting for us to get it. "Don't you see, guys? Jack was a military man. It's the metric system. The C is for centimeters, the M for meters, and the K for kilometers."

"Wow, that fits," I said and walked to the colonel's oversized desk to write the math problem out on a piece of paper. I substituted the measurements for the letters, but it didn't make any more sense than it did before. "I still don't get it. With the metric system added you have ten minus sixteen, plus twenty

Chapter Twenty-Six - The Metric System

centimeters, plus thirty meters, equals ten kilometers. Are these map coordinates or something?"

"That's what I thought," Tim said as he, Katie, and Jesse came over to the desk and pondered my scribblings. We each took turns trying to do the math in a way that made it work but failed. I was the first to give up and went back to Colonel Bandershot's "I love me" wall. It was impressive.

"Jesse, do you know what all this stuff is?" I asked.

Jesse pointed to what looked like a metal soup bowl on the table. "Well, that's a World War One helmet, and I guess you recognize the pistol and grenade."

Tim joined us. "What's the big green box and all these bullet holders?"

Jesse came over and pointed at the centerpiece of the collection. "You see that rifle up there? That's an M1 Garand, the standard U.S. Army infantry rifle of World War Two. It was what we did all our killing with before we got the M-16 we use today. The bullets you see on the table go with that and they're held in a clip with eight bullets or rounds. The M-16 uses different bullets carried in what we call a magazine or 'mag' for short. The M-16 mags can hold up to 30 rounds. Oh, and we grunts call that green box a can, it's short for ammo can. That's what the bullets come in."

Tim looked down at the paper he had in his hand. It was his version of the math problem. Then he got a distant look on his face as he sat in one of the high-back leather wing chairs that framed the wall.

"Sixteen, magazines, and cans," he mumbled.

"What did you say?" I asked

Tim stood and walked back to the desk. "Sixteen, magazines, and cans."

He grabbed a fresh sheet of paper and started writing. After a few seconds, he set down his pencil and called us over.

"It isn't a math problem; it's a shopping list."

We all leaned forward for a clear view of Tim's work.

"Twenty C stands for twenty cans, ammo cans, and thirty M means thirty magazines," Tim said while pointing to the weapons on the other side of the room.

"And the top numbers—ten minus sixteen—isn't subtraction; it means the buyer wanted ten M-16 rifles," I added, having broken the code, too.

Jesse picked up the piece of paper. "And all of it was available at Inversol's market—the armory's bunker."

"Bingo!" Tim said. "And Katie, you were close. The letters aren't metric, but the K does stand for kilo. Kilo means one thousand in Greek, and in this case, it represents the price of the items on the shopping list. Jack Inversol was going to sell everything to Ed Stickley for a bargain basement price of ten K or ten thousand dollars."

"This was the deal Inversol felt guilty about," I said. "He was going to sell a terrorist enough military weapons to kill a building full of people."

Chapter Twenty-Six - The Metric System

"But he changed his mind and planned to 'make amends,' just as he wrote in his note," Katie added. "Except Stickley stopped him and helped him overdose on morphine."

"But wait. If Jack overdosed on morphine, how did he write the fraternity letters at the bottom of his note? Stickley wouldn't let him do that," I said.

Tim put his arm around Katie. "That's where Stickley made his big mistake. He thought Jack was dead when he left him slumped on his desk, but he was wrong. Jack was stronger than Stickley imagined or maybe better words would be more tolerant. Jack's been abusing morphine for years, and the body builds up a tolerance for anything you take in quantity, be it beer, antibiotics, even morphine."

Katie wiped a tear from her eye and asked, "So Jack came to after Stickley left?"

"It would explain the strange stain and line at the bottom of the suicide note. When Jack passed out, his fountain pen stopped moving, and the paper drew ink from the nib, causing the stain. As he came to, his arm moved, causing the pen to drag across the paper drawing the line. Then with his last bit of strength, he identified his killer by copying what he saw on Stickley's tie clip: Delta Phi."

Katie dropped into her dad's desk chair. "It all makes sense. Jack knew what he was doing was wrong and stopped."

"Crap!" Tim yelled. "We forgot to tell you what we found at the cave tonight. It may tie in with what we just figured out. We need to go back to the armory, and we need to go now."

Chapter Twenty-Seven
Back to the Armory

No one wanted to take the traumatized VW bus, so we piled into the Eldorado. Katie was the last one out of the house after grabbing two flashlights. Her tears were gone, and her face was steeled with determination as she jumped into the driver's seat and started the car. Before I could brace myself, she applied the accelerator with even more vigor than during my first ride.

"Why did you go to the armory earlier?" I asked Tim.

"The metric system," he said as he turned around to look at Jesse and me in the back seat. "Just like you, I thought the kilometers thing might be directions, and I know the military uses them instead of miles, so I hoped we might find a map or something to make sense of them."

We all inhaled as Katie avoided braking at an intersection by swerving up onto the sidewalk to pass a car. "Of course, we didn't find anything. We didn't even get into the armory. The tennis group was there again."

"Jeez, Katie! Try to get us there in one piece," Tim exclaimed.

Katie's face pouted as she slowed down a little. "We parked where we always do and started down the hill to see if we could sneak in through the back door, but then we saw the wires."

"Wires?" I asked.

Chapter Twenty-Seven - Back to the Armory

Katie smiled and hit the accelerator again, charging the Eldorado up the road to the armory. "Yes, wires. They were on the path to the cave."

Tim pointed out the windshield to the dark end of the road ahead. "There were two wires—yellow and red—and they were twisted together. We followed them, and they led us to a pickup truck hidden behind a pile of wood at the end of the street. The truck was locked, but we could see the wires weren't attached to anything. They were just looped on the passenger seat, so we followed them in the other direction, and they went right into the cave."

"That's when it got really weird," Katie said as she slammed on the brakes right in front of the stacked wood. "When we entered the cave, we heard something we shouldn't have been able to hear."

Jesse leaned forward. "What?"

"Tennis," Tim answered. "We heard the guys in the armory playing tennis. We could hear the balls bouncing and the sneakers squeaking—everything. With no flashlight we couldn't see much, so we went home to get one, and that's when we met you."

Jesse's face was a question mark. "You could hear what was going on in the armory from the cave?"

"Yeah," said Katie. "It was bizarre."

"Let's see the wires," I said as I pushed on the back of Tim's seat, encouraging him to get out.

The armory was dark and the rain had stopped, but clouds blocked the moonlight, so I turned on a flashlight.

Tim had the other one. "Over here," he called as he stood about twenty yards in front of the car.

The wires were slim but stiff, not flexible like extension cord wire. Just as Tim said, they ended at the pickup. There was nothing else in the truck, and the license plate was local.

"Let's see what they're connected to," Jesse said as he took the flashlight from Tim and shined it on the wires.

They followed the path we had taken many times through the woods, to the edge of the cliff, and then down the steep pathway to the entrance of the cave, but they didn't end where we had our parties. They continued into the darkness.

We all paused and stared into the black—now suddenly foreboding back of the cave.

"I don't hear anything," Jesse said.

Tim pushed him aside and continued to follow the wires. "That's because there's nothing to hear. The armory's empty."

We reached the back of the cave and quickly saw why Katie and Tim could hear the tennis game. Someone had been busy back there—busy digging. On the left side was a semi-professional-looking four-by-four-foot tunnel reinforced with the lumber I'd seen during my last visit.

Chapter Twenty-Seven - Back to the Armory

Jesse crouched down and used his flashlight to illuminate the tunnel. "This ain't no mole hole. This took some know-how and serious work to dig. It reminds me of the Viet Cong tunnels in Nam. They once took us mess hall guys out to see one after they cleared it out."

The tunnel wasn't long, maybe twenty feet, and ended at a concrete brick wall that had been broken open. Beyond it lay storage boxes with white letters and numbers painted on their sides.

"That's the ammo bunker," Jesse said pointing into the tunnel. "Someone figured out that this cave is deep enough that it would only take a short tunnel to reach the bunker. This must be how Jack and Stickley were going to get the ammunition out without being seen."

"But what's with the wires?" Tim asked as he took the flashlight out of my hand and entered the tunnel.

Katie was right behind him. I looked at Jesse.

"What the hell?" he said, and we ducked down and followed.

The tunnel engulfed me in darkness with only an occasional beam of light slipping past Jesse's frame as he struggled to squeeze through. The smell of damp dirt filled my nose, and the sound of shuffling feet echoed in my ears. As I neared the end, I heard Tim say, "See if you can find a light switch."

As Jesse stood, I poked my head through the shattered concrete bricks. I heard a click and another voice say, "Will this do," as the room filled with light.

Slippery When Wet

Katie gasped, and Jesse said, "You!"

It was Stickley.

The smug look was back on his face, but the rest of him looked like he'd been rode hard and put away wet. His left arm hung limply at his side, and there was matted blood in his hair above a nasty open wound. His right hand clutched his pistol, and he used it to direct us to move together.

"You're just in time to help me finish the job Sergeant Inversol and I started. It's pickup day, but after our little bus ride and my walk back from West Virginia, I'm a bit under the weather." Stickley's eyes grew wide, and he started giggling uncontrollably, then laughed out loud. "Under the weather! I'm a Weathermen, and I'm under the weather. Ha!"

We did not laugh with him.

The bunker was about the size of a three-car garage and had a curved corrugated metal roof. Three of the walls were concrete brick. The other was all iron bars with a jail-like door in its center. Beyond that was a hallway with a single metal door. Boxes and ammo cans lined the walls. Stickley stood behind several of them that had been moved to the center of the room. Sitting on the boxes was what I recognized as an explosive's detonator.

"Little girl," Stickley said as he pointed his gun at Katie. "Come over here."

Both Jesse and Tim stepped in front of Katie, and Stickley began to giggle again. "How noble but futile. Gentlemen, if

Chapter Twenty-Seven - Back to the Armory

you don't move, I'll put a bullet through both you and the girl." He choked on his last word and began to cough. His face tensed in pain.

Katie pushed through the boys and walked towards Stickley. "We need to do as he says."

"Smart girl. Stand right there in front of the boxes," Stickley said, pointing to where he wanted her. "Now the rest of you, I need you to carry these out to the pickup truck. I'll stay here with this pretty young thing to guarantee your return. You have forty-five minutes starting now."

"Let me guess, there are ten M-16s, twenty cans of ammunition, and thirty magazines in these boxes," Tim said.

"I'm impressed. You guys are brighter than the average idiots in this Godforsaken town. That was the deal Jack and I had," Stickley started to say, but the cough returned, and he faltered. Steadying himself against the wall, Stickley continued, "After the Pentagon bombing, our cell split up to wait until things calmed down. I've been hiding out here working Inversol to get supplies for our next job. Do you know I gave that slob a down payment of three thousand dollars, and all he planned to do with it was buy morphine? What a loser, but I guess he was worried he'd have trouble finding drugs in Costa Rica."

I could see anger building in Katie's eyes as her hands became fists.

Slippery When Wet

Stickley nodded in the direction of one of the wider boxes labeled M67s. "With the sergeant gone, I've added a bit to the deal. The colonel's death got me interested in grenades, and I've decided to take a few with me, so that adds to the boxes you need to move. Too bad the good sergeant is no longer around to accept his final payment."

Katie spat at Stickley. It landed on his scratched and muddy Delta Phi tie tack.

"Careful, little girl. If you're not nice, I'll take you with me and introduce you to some of my friends who will make you do things even your mommy won't do."

Katie spat again, but it fell harmlessly to the floor.

"That's right, I saw the pictures Inversol had of your mom and her oversexed buddies, but your friends already know that," Stickley said.

Katie looked at Tim. Tim pointed at me.

Stickley turned the gun in my direction. "Give me back the photo I left in the bus."

I pulled the damp picture from my back pocket and held it out for Stickley.

Katie grabbed it.

Stickley giggled again. "Go ahead, little girl. I don't mind if you see what fun your mom was having."

Chapter Twenty-Seven - Back to the Armory

Katie looked at the picture then back at Stickley. "Well, at least that's the Pat Bandershot I know—on top and in control."

Stickley stepped forward and took it. "Inversol was going to destroy them, but I thought it would be better to leave them behind. And to think the older generation frowns on the hippies' free love. What hypocrites. Now get moving, boys. You've only got forty minutes left."

I glanced up at the wall clock hanging over the jail-like barred door to the bunker—1972 was in its last hour. "Okay, this is going to take a few trips. Jesse, can you handle two smaller boxes on your own? Tim and I will get one of the big ones."

"Yeah, I've got them," Jesse said as he grabbed the handle on the side of the two boxes labeled 5.56mm ammunition and dragged them to the tunnel's opening.

Tim and I picked up a crate of M-16s and followed him. It took us six trips to get all the boxes into the back of the truck. On the last one, Jesse hoisted a box on his shoulders, and one under his arm as Tim dragged the grenade box. I struggled with one labeled MAGAZINES.

Stickley was seated on a box near the door when we returned, and he was dabbing his head wound with a handkerchief. He was visibly weaker than before. Katie stood to his side with her arms crossed and a scowl on her face.

"Whoever dug this tunnel knew what they were doing to keep that twenty feet of Cumberland topsoil from crashing down on us," Jesse said leaning forward with his hands on his knees. Sweat poured from his brow.

Stickley looked at the tunnel's opening and giggled. "I dug every inch of that damn thing myself over the past two weeks. I was a civil engineering major at the University of Michigan, but I never thought my contribution to construction would be in mining. It's a pity I have to close it all up now."

"What do you mean?" Katie asked.

He waved his gun indicating he wanted us to move away from the tunnel's opening. "I want you all on the other side of those bars. Little girl, open the door, please."

Katie moved to the barred door and pulled it open, and we all walked into the hallway that separated the bunker from the rest of the armory. The area was small and had a door on the other side that I assumed led to the gym.

Staying inside the bunker and holstering his gun in his pant waist, Stickley pushed the door shut and locked it with a key. Then he shuffled towards a box on the side of the bunker. He dragged his left foot behind him with each pained, uneasy step.

I saw Jesse try the door to the stairs. Finding it locked, he went to the end of the hall and looked around near a stand of lockers.

Stickley finished getting a few more clips of ammunition for his handgun then picked up the detonator.

"Hey, you can't just leave us here!" Tim shouted.

Chapter Twenty-Seven - Back to the Armory

"Don't worry, you won't have long to wait," Stickley said as he pointed to a box on the floor labeled C-4 EXPLOSIVES. The box had the red and yellow wires coming out of it.

"I just need to hook the other end of those up to my detonator, and all your troubles will be over."

Stickley giggled again, hobbled towards the tunnel, ducked, and was gone.

I looked at the gray walls of the bunker and shivered, realizing for the first time how cold it was. With no windows and only the harsh lighting from two bare bulbs, the space seemed to shrink around me as I stared through the iron bars at the red and yellow wires. I could hear the clock ticking.

Chapter Twenty-Eight
Up on the Roof

I was still staring at the red and yellow wires as the clock grew louder with every second.

"Okay, don't lose it," I said to myself. "There has got to be a way out of here."

I looked around for something to use as a lever. Maybe I could pry open the cell door. The hall between the bunker's bars and the entrance to the gym was a shallow ten by twenty feet, and the only exit was the door to the stairs. To my left were a fire extinguisher and storage bins. I was about to open one of the bins when there was a tremendous crash. I turned in the direction of the noise and saw Jesse had tipped over the stand of lockers at the other end of the hall.

"Not that it matters, but I found where Inversol hid after Major Bennington shot him," Jesse said. "Look here."

Behind the overturned lockers was an opening cut into the concrete block wall that led to a small alcove dug into the hillside.

Jesse looked into the opening. "I always wondered where Inversol disappeared to during drill."

"Can we get out from in there?" Tim asked as he stepped into the hole with his flashlight.

"No, it's just a hideout with a mattress, a Coleman lantern, and some bloodstained paper towels," Jesse said.

Chapter Twenty-Eight - Up on the Roof

Tim reemerged from the hole. "Well, there are two other things. Look what was under the mattress." Tim held up a half-empty pint of Jack Daniel's and an inch-thick stack of one-hundred-dollar bills.

"That's got to be the three thousand dollars Stickley was whining about," Jesse said while Tim fanned through the bills.

"Guys, do I need to remind you that we are running out of time?" I asked with nervousness creeping into my voice.

"Can we use these to open the door?" Tim reached into the interior pockets of his pea-coat and removed two M67 grenades. "I got them out of that last box I schlepped out to the truck. I'm sure Stickley won't miss them."

Jesse held up his hands like he was trying to catch a basketball. "Don't you remember what happened to the colonel. Grenades detonated in confined spaces do nasty things to people. Even if it blows open the door without killing us, it might set off the other ammunition in the bunker, bringing the entire armory down."

Tim put the grenades back into his pockets. "Oh, right. Bad idea, huh?"

There was the sound of a key turning and a lock releasing as Katie said with exasperation, "Men!" She had used her copy of her dad's master key to unlock the door to the stairwell.

Immediately accepting the superiority of women, we followed her up the stairs and into the gym. Flipping on the lights, we raced to the front door but found it blocked with chains. It was the same for the other exits, and we realized we hadn't escaped our jail cell—it just got bigger.

Katie made a whimpering sound and dropped to her knees. "We're trapped."

"The roof! We can get up on the roof above the first-floor offices and should be able to get down from there," Jesse said as he ran down the hall past Inversol's office and into the breakroom. "Help me get this table into the hall. With a chair on it we can reach the hatch in the ceiling."

I looked up at the clock on the gym's wall. I figured four or five minutes had passed since Stickley left the tunnel. "Hurry, Stickley's got to be back to the truck by now."

Tim and I helped get the table into the hall, and Katie dragged a chair out. In less than a minute, we were all on the roof looking in the direction of the pickup truck. The clouds had cleared, and a lantern of a full moon hung in the winter sky.

The truck was still there, but we didn't see Stickley at first. Then we spotted him as he emerged from the woods. He was having trouble walking. His gait was uneven, and he was dragging his left foot more than before.

"We've got to stop him," Katie said. "Jesse, can you throw a grenade that far?"

Jesse stared into the darkness, judging the distance. "That's got to be at least one hundred yards; there's no way I can get a grenade close. A Frisbee maybe, but not a grenade."

Chapter Twenty-Eight - Up on the Roof

"That's it!" I yelled and dropped back down through the hatch and into the break room. There I scooped up the stack of record albums and the roll of duct tape.

Jesse was leaning down through the hatch as I came back into the hallway and I yelled to him, "Catch!" as I tossed the duct tape then the LPs up to him.

"What are you going to do with those?" Katie asked as Jesse dropped the records and tape onto the roof.

"Make Frisbees," Jesse said.

"Grenade-carrying Frisbees," I added as I pulled myself back up through the hatch.

Jesse was already ripping open the LP covers, and Tim tore off strips of duct tape and stuck them to his pant leg.

"Okay, we need to be smart about this," Jesse said as he held an LP in his hand. We can't tape over the arming pin. He wobbled the album up and down. "It's also a bit flimsy. I think we are going to need two LPs or maybe three per Frisbee."

Tim handed Jesse another LP, and he oriented the grenade so that the arming pin stood straight up. "I'll hold it, Tim, while you use the tape to secure the grenade. Has Stickley made it to the truck yet?"

I stared out into the darkness. "He's close. Hurry."

We heard the pickup's door open, and a dome light turned on in the cab. "He's there!"

Jesse stood and held his homemade flying bomb aloft. The tape covered most of the grenade. It looked like a model of the flying saucer from the movie *The Day the Earth Stood Still.*

Jesse held the edge of the LP tightly in his right hand and took a few practice swings as Tim started work on another saucer bomb.

"I don't know. It's a bit heavier than I'm used to."

"Throw it, Jesse. Throw it now. We're out of time!" Katie pleaded.

Jesse decided on the traditional Frisbee throw and positioned himself at the edge of the roof at the point with the most direct line to the target. He curled the disk in towards his chest then slowly extended his arm out fully—aiming it at the distant truck.

Then, after a moment of stillness, he pulled the pin from the grenade and threw the disk with almost Herculean effort. It disappeared immediately into the darkness between the armory and Stickley, and we waited.

The disk hit the ground and skipped forward a few times—then exploded. The sky lit up like the Fourth of July, and dirt clods fell like heavy rain all around it. But the throw was short and to the right, completely missing the truck.

Our bomb got Stickley's attention, and we watched as he got out of the truck and pulled his pistol. Shots fired in our direction, and we all ducked as bullets ricocheted off the wall of the armory. I heard Jesse curse under his breath.

Chapter Twenty-Eight - Up on the Roof

"Last one," Tim said as he handed another grenade Frisbee to Jesse who was crouching beside him. "I used three LPs on this one."

Jesse stood and looked at the pickup again.

I put my hand on Jesse's shoulder. "You can do it. Try your overhand throw. It's a killer."

Jesse looked at the disk then back at me, and with a slight smile and a wink of his eye, he said, "It's cool." He turned back towards the truck.

Stickley fired his pistol again, and everyone ducked—except Jesse. He stood like a statue focused on his target holding in his hand our last chance to stop a madman. Jesse cocked his wrist out to the right as if the LPs were a tennis racket. Then he swung it back and forth a few times, focusing all his strength and Frisbee-tossing talent into one perfect throw. Then—he pulled the pin and, in one smooth yet powerful motion, sent the grenade-carrying disk flying into the night air.

Chapter Twenty-Nine
Happy New Year

Katie, Jesse, and I stood shivering on the roof of the armory. The air was filled with sirens and flashing lights as police and firefighters arrived. Tim had dropped back down into the armory to call for help.

A fireman's ladder banged against the side of the building, and two police officers, with guns drawn, joined us on the roof.

"Okay, boys and girls. What's going on up here?"

Tim popped his head up through the hatch. "I got a hold of my dad at the country club and told him everything. He's bringing help."

One of the policemen pulled Tim onto the roof. "Why don't you tell me everything, too." And we did.

The police and firefighters thought they were responding to the misuse of New Year's Eve fireworks but instead found an unexploded ordnance situation it would take five EOD specialists to handle.

Despite our rational explanations, we were all handcuffed and prepared for transport to the police station when Doctor Lewis, Mort Peskin, Frankie Adams, and my dad arrived. Oh, and Mayor Ed Conklin showed up, too, dressed in a tux. He was acting chief of police with Thompkins gone.

Chapter Twenty-Nine - Happy New Year

After the police confirmed our story with Mort and Frankie, they removed the handcuffs, and we all walked to the pickup truck which was now ablaze in spotlights and cordoned off with crime scene tape.

I would like to believe Stickley saw the grenade-carrying LP as it landed near him a second before it exploded, but I'll never know. According to the coroner, the truck door spared his body, but it didn't stop a razor-sharp metal fragment from piercing his left eye and ricocheting around in his brain.

There he was, dead on the front seat with the detonator in his hand and the eight-by-ten-inch black-and-white photo of the mayor and Pat Bandershot lying beside him.

One-Shot Charlie appeared out of nowhere and got the perfect picture of a police officer handing Mayor Conklin the photo.

Unfortunately, Stickley was not the only victim of the explosion. The grenade also peppered the Eldorado with hot metal. It looked worse than Jesse's bus.

Information found in Stickley's apartment led to the arrest of two other members of his terrorist cell, and with the signing of the 1973 Vietnam Peace Accord a few weeks later, the Weathermen Underground disintegrated as a threat and became just a smudge on an ugly page of history.

We all enjoyed the spotlight, but Jesse received the most recognition, and rightly so. He was a hero, and the local newspaper played it up big. In the article detailing the events was an interview with Jesse and his dad.

Slippery When Wet

"Mr. Preslor, to what do you attribute your son's heroism?"

"That's the Sally in him," Mr. Preslor answered and proceeded to fill two columns of newsprint with the story of Sally's successful escape to freedom one hundred and fifteen years earlier. The reporter quoted Jesse as saying, "I'm proud of my Grandma Sally and all the other brave people who fought for freedom."

The article was picked up by the *Associated Press*, and Walter Cronkite even mentioned Jesse on the *CBS Evening News*, calling him the Frisbee-grenade guardsman.

The Maryland National Guard promoted Jesse to sergeant and awarded him a college scholarship which allowed him to transfer to the University of Maryland as a full-time student.

Katie, Tim, and I failed to tell the police about the three thousand dollars we found in Inversol's hiding place, and we all agreed that Jesse should use it to buy a new VW bus.

Pat Bandershot replaced her dead Eldorado with a Ford Pinto, sold her mansion, and moved into a modest pink-brick home near Allegany so that Katie could walk to school.

On January nineteenth, Tim, Katie, and I went to the Allegany winter dance. Joni returned to Cumberland as my date, and we all had a grand time. Near the end of the dance, Katie asked, "Would it be okay with you if we all went up to the armory? I'm missing Jack and my dad."

Tim had a six-pack of beer chilling in his station wagon, and we ended the evening at the cliff above the cave toasting our detective work and the loved ones lost.

Chapter Twenty-Nine - Happy New Year

My life went back to normal, and I was glad. Senior year of high school is supposed to be special, and mine was just starting. It would be tough for 1973 to top 1972.

A week later, Reverend Cooper organized a special Sunday church service at Emmanuel to commemorate the end of the Vietnam War and the second inauguration of President Nixon.

I was the crucifer again and was standing near Reverend Cooper as he led the congregation in the celebration. Jesse was all decked out in his new sergeant's stripes leading a contingent from the National Guard, and his proud father sat right beside him. Katie, Tim, and Mrs. Bandershot were in the front pew, and the rest of the church was filled with most of the same Cumberland dignitaries who attended the unveiling of the colonel's tank three months earlier—except for Mayor Conklin. He had resigned two days earlier.

"Let us rejoice and give thanks unto the Lord for all he has given us," Reverend Cooper intoned.

"Amen," replied the congregation.

"The nightmare of Vietnam is over, giving way to a time of healing. The nation has a bright future ahead of it and the stability of President Nixon's second term to assure us time to heal."

Reverend Cooper moved down in front of the pews. "The turbulent 1960s are behind us. Let us embrace the spirit of a new age of peace and prosperity."

His voice gathered steam as he rolled into a sing-song litany of prose.

"I challenge you—every one of you—to turn a page, discard the old, and think anew."

To drive home his point, he walked back up the steps to the beautifully embellished brass lectern and put his hand on the ancient *King James Bible*.

"The past is past—your past is passed—let it go, and embrace the new. This book may be full of wisdom, but it's hard to read. The language is old and stilted. I have ordered a modern interpretation of the Bible to replace it, and we will use it together as we move forward."

He grabbed both sides of the spare-tire-sized book and lifted it over his head.

The envelope I hid under the Bible hung on for as long as it could, but when the reverend swung the book up, the force was too great, and the envelope flew out over the congregation, releasing its contents.

As the key club photos fluttered down on the now transfixed parishioners, I quietly leaned my crucifer's cross against the wall and left through Sally's tunnel.

Acknowledgments

Writing a book is fun and very rewarding, but editing a book is hard work. That's why I got lots of help when it was time to make my prose presentable. That help fell into several categories. First, there was story development. I had an idea, but it was my lovely wife Karen Syckes, who added creative twists and historical tie-ins that made the story special. She also tackled the miserable job of being the first editor, which she did with talent, tenacity, and tact. Thank you, and I love you. My best friend and main character Tim Lewis also helped me shape the storyline and provided much needed technical expertise on all things Army. Paul Ryan then helped me structure the prose and provided the first formal edit. Next came the proofreaders, and I'm eternally grateful to, Stan and Steve Syckes, Vicki Hancock, Kirk Adkins, Kris and Dave Poling, Marian and Mark Saterfield, Larry and Sandy Mackereth, and finally local Cumberland historian Al Feldstein. Al was kind enough also to write a foreword. Finally, I am glad I used the super editing services of Kelly Hartigan (XterraWeb) at editing.xterraweb.com. Thank you one and all.

Made in the USA
Columbia, SC
16 August 2019